First Printed 2025
Available in e-book and paperback
from Kindle Direct Publishing

# Charlie's Last Corn on the Cob

## The Brighton Job

With thanks to the excellent screen writer Troy Kennedy Martin, born in Bute, died in Ditchling for 'The Italian Job' and to Michael Caine for his handsome portrayal of Charlie Croker in that same film.

And to them film critics what thought it right and proper to give that 1960s classic just three stars – and in perpetuity mind – what was you thinking?!

# Chapter 1

Now, if you has ever been down them '*Lanes*' in Brighton, you will know that they is a warren of small-time jewellers, tourist fripperies, and a load of old tatt. And normally, on a nice summer's day like today, they'd be buzzing with flocks of the gullible - as I calls them - but not this morning. No, them streets is quiet. And a number of them jewellers' shops has got on display the same identical printed sign;

'*Closed – as a mark of respect*'

Well, obviously, a job lot's been done, and them posters has all been passed around with instructions. That's right, the Fitzpatricks is wanting to just make sure everyone is showing the required respect.

Still, it don't stop a neat young saxophonist and his drummer mate on a pair of brushes oozing out a nice little improvisation job on that old Matt Munroe number '*On days like these*'. 'Though not much chance of any generous contributions from passers-by today mind; streets being empty and that. But that's young buskers for you. They live in hope, don't they?

And the reason for this picture of, well, obliging respectfulness if you will, can be found in a churchyard not far from *The Lanes*. Our Lady of the Immaculate Conception - The 'Maculate Concept', as we calls it - even if not much of the immaculate is on display today. No, just a load of old third-rate, Brighton and South London gangsters assembled in small groups, heads nodding, small talking, hands shaking, other parts shaking too, you know the old Parkinson's. Crumbling codger villains, held up with sticks.

Now, as your anonymous narrator of this and many other tales, I'm familiar enough with the drill. You know, introduce a few key characters first, then layer the others on top. Keep it tight and pace it, don't make it confusing. And make sure to chuck in a big crash-bang-wallop early on to secure the reader's ongoing attention. But I mean, what have we got here? A bloody funeral. And like, everybody's there. I mean, the whole bloody cast. Well, I can hardly ignore them, can I? No. So, I'll keep it as brief as I can, and you should get the hang of who's who and what's what as we go along. It's not complicated. And even though it's a funeral, well, it's one full of crooks innit, so things should liven up soon enough.

Anyhows, a large black Transit van comes into the churchyard. It's not the usual *Graves R Us*! hearse. Strange that. More a service vehicle, though it's tidy enough I suppose, and been washed clean for the purpose. The Transit is followed by three of them disability vans; one red, one white and the other one blue.

Young Reg is behind the wheel of the first one, Spandau Barry drives the second, and Kyrstee the third.

Good looking boy, Reg. Neat, tight, well-built, handy too, an excellent mechanic. He pulls up into the first disabled parking space.

Spandau Barry parks up in the second. Got that podgy, getting-on-a-bit good looks has Spandau Barry, you know, a bit Simon Le Bon. What makes sense since Barry - a Brummie by birth and disposition - is also well trapped in the 1980s New Romantic movement. So, he's got a sort of highland wrap around him. Unusually though, for an old New Romantic, he's always got that parrot, Hadley on his shoulder too. What with his blue and yellow plumage - nice bright colours - Hadley looks like a sunny day.

Charlie's latest young bird - the human kind that is - Kyrstee, parks up in the third disabled parking space. Sweet-natured thing is young Kyrstee. Nice face, lovely figure. Hair colour might come from a bottle but being as she is in the business, she makes a very good job of it. And the rest of her, well, it's all natural, the real thing, you know. None of that weird plastic-silicone injection and implant look what is so common nowadays. You know, them young folks what looks like they's been assembled by some shyster surgeon what just scraped a D Minus at medical night school.

Anyhows, Spandau gets out first, opens the back door and out in reverse drive comes Lenny in his mobility scooter what carries a car registration plate 848 CRY. Lenny might be pushing on a bit - well, like the rest of us - but he's still got the style. You know, Jamaican good looks, the dreadlock pony tail might be grey, but it's still dreadlocks, and them rimless glasses, gives him a sort of intelligent look. Devoted to old Lenny is Spandau, not in a sexual way, least I don't think so, but, well, like a lot of gay men are. You know, suited to looking after other people.

Then Reg does the same with his rear van door and out pops Chen. South Asian ethnic extraction is Chen. Small, slight, well you know them South Asians, never crease. I mean, could be anywhere between 50 and 80 years old, lucky sod. Always wears a vest, does Chen. Feels the cold, see. Daft on ghosts and spirits and all that nonsense too. His mobility scooter wears the plate LGW 453, and it makes a particularly annoying beep in reverse.

Finally, it is the turn of the man himself and the ever-sexy Kyrstee opens the rear door to reveal Charlie Crystal. She struggles a bit with that door. Not that it's difficult, just that, well, Kyrstee's not the sharpest pair of scissors in the vanity case. Anyhows, out zips Charlie head on. Mobility vehicle's in nice shape. 163 ELT on the plate.

Still got a good head of hair on him has old Charlie, even if it is lambswool white, and still got a faceful of well-earned good looks too. Well, I mean pop a pair of them signature black-rimmed specs on him and you might be forgiven for thinking he was Michael Caine himself. But it's the classic teardrop glasses for Charlie Crystal today and every day. And on this particular day - naturally - they is sunglasses. Well, shades is always a good look at a funeral. Same goes for the black tie. Mind you, not quite sure what's with the bow tie variety. Though I suppose for Charlie Crystal, the passing of Peter Fitzpatrick is cause for celebration, and as such he should dress accordingly.

So, Charlie is also sporting his black sheen-shimmer suit, though the trousers is cut extra loose from the knee down. This is on account of him having to carry a bag of his own piss around strapped to his leg, courtesy of a very angry prostate. Yeah, that little gland is intent on taking him sharpish to his grave. Still, today is special and in addition to his smart suit and bow tie, Charlie wears a big grin. What's that about? I mean, we all know what he's got up his trouser leg, but what's he got up his sleeve?

Contrast Charlie's cheerful countenance with the resentful stare of Brenda Fitzpatrick, who is not happy. Well, is she ever? That pale Irish boat-race, zig-zag lined with a deeply etched, criss-cross geometry from a lifetime of frowning and scowling. I tell you; Pythagoras couldn't figure that one out. Her look of misery is underlined by a couple of petulant streaks of bright scarlet lipstick slashed right across her thin lips. She don't like to be kept waiting does Brenda, not by no-one, especially old Charlie Crystal. Today, as a mark of respect to her big brother - the dead one that is, Peter, not his twin, Paddy. No, no respect for him - it's the black dress, black half-veil, black highish heels. Well, she is pushing on a bit now and you might say she should be racing on the flat. 'Specially since she's got a big cheese and onion on that right foot. Booked in for a private job down the Montefiori soon as the company stock take is over and done.

Brenda gives Paddy the nod and Paddy snaps his fingers. Paddy likes to think that we all believe that he's in charge now. As if. Not even his own boy, Paddy Junior, thinks that. And that's a lad what in his thirties still can't figure out his right from his left. You know, struggles to get his shoes on proper of a morning.

Reg, Kyrstee, Barry, and Chen on his scooter makes their ways into the Maculate Concept with them other 'respectful' mourners. Whilst Charlie and Lenny line up their mobility scooters at the front of the pall bearers. The lead undertaker from *Graves R Us!*, top hat and all - who's he fooling? - fits a wooden plank across them scooters. Well, they is a fair size them vehicles, none of your Toytown jobs.

Then the top hat geezer directs his lackeys to lift out the coffin from that black Transit. I say coffin, but it's a weird throne-shaped thing. Tall and heavy too. Hence the big van. You'd never fit that in a normal hearse. They place the back of this strange coffin thing on the plank what's across them scooters. Then the four other pall bearers, Paddy and Paddy's young lad, Paddy junior, and two other crooks from the Fitzpatrick crew fall in behind. And they all has to crouch down to accommodate the difference in height from the scooters. I mean, you'd think they might have practised this routine before, or at least had the gumption to work it out on the back of a fag packet. But that's *Graves R Us!* for you; no attention to detail.

Up in the choir loft, a fourpiece: organ, electric guitar, drum and base - what's members is all dressed up in colourful purple velvet - starts up with Booker T's *Green Onions*. And down the aisle the procession goes to this musical accompaniment. And they's all stuttering and wobbling as they try to hold up that ridiculous coffin. A smirking Charlie gives his scooter the odd rev just to liven up proceedings. Though being electric, it don't make much noise.

On arrival at the altar, them undertaker lackeys lift and place the weird throne-shaped coffin on the tiled floor. Paddy and his mugs file into the front pews on one side with the rest of the Fitzpatrick clan, and Charlie and Lenny scoot round the other to join their lot. And look who's behind them, the original team: Mickey, Coffee-mate, Big Albie, Bas, Pinkie and Trevor. Get that cap off our head Trevor! You're in church!

Well, it's just like them old days, even if a few of them geezers looks a little bit worse for wear. Well, time marches on, as I says. But some've brought their young ones along too. You know, the next crooked generation.

*Green Onions* comes to a close, tricky really, 'cause by rights it should fade out, and old Father Scanlon - yes, he's still alive - steps up to the pulpit.

Now, whilst we is on the subject of doppelgangers, if Charlie has had that old 'Michael Caine's evil twin' millstone hanging round his neck all these years, just imagine this.

Imagine if 'The King of Rock and Roll' - yeah him - had not succumbed to Las Vegas excess and instead lived to a ripe old age, maybe become a bit confused, developed a thick Irish accent, and what do you know, joined the priesthood. Well, this might be just how he would look - a ringer for Father Scanlon - or vices versa… You know, the thick sideburns, slicked back grey hair, lip going up at one side for no good reason.

Yeah, I know, strange innit? One story with two lookie-likies. Mind you, Brighton is a place full of people who ain't exactly what they is pretending to be.

He's got a couple of young altar boys in tow has Old Father Scanlon; one carrying a large crucifix stuck on a pole and the other swinging a smoking thurible. I suspect The King would have swapped them for a couple of tasty birds in bikinis, but that's religion for you. Bikinis is not an option. Not in public anyhows. And the high priest of the Maculate Concept is dressed in particularly flamboyant vestments today: bright whites, golds, edges clipped with silver. Looks like he's just about to celebrate mass in Caesar's Palace.

And there you have it. It's a lot of new faces to get your head around, as I says. I know, but you'll pick it up as we go along. And I reckon I've set the scene good and proper.

So, now to the story. For you don't want me rabbiting on all the time, do you? See, I'm just an observer. Fly on the wall, that's me. Fly on the wall.

…

## Chapter 2

"Ah now, lads," says Father Scanlon, "lovely music, lovely music. The food of love, is it? The food of love! And who was it said that, now? Is it in the bible? No, no. Sure, haven't I read that book many times myself? I'd know. Or was it Elvis? Yes, yes, I think it was Elvis; a very saintly man in his own way, you know. And what was it called?"

The old priest shuffles his dementia-friendly prompt cards.

"*Green Onions*? Ah, yes, sure…. And what could be more appropriate for a funeral than a plate of err… than a… for the funeral of…"

Charlie turns to Lenny with a smile. "Looks very promising, Len. Old Father Scanlon's on fine demented form today."

"For we are here," continues the priest, "gathered not to mourn a death, no, but to celebrate…"

"He speaks for us all!" pipes up Charlie.

See, I told you - celebration - that's what it is for Charlie.

"Shh, Charlie!" says Kyrstee, sitting behind him.

Old Father Scanlon carries on; don't notice, see. "Not to celebrate a death, but a life!"

No reaction, no nodding heads, just stares. To be fair, the priest reads the situation.

"Well, now, I know it's a cliché, sure," says Father Scanlon, "and haven't I used it many times before myself? Well, I'm eighty-three you know, that's a lot of funerals. Why, if I had a penny for every cliché I've uttered…"

Charlie turns to Lenny again, "Does he write this stuff himself?"

Spandau Barry leans forwards, taps Charlie on the back, then whispers. "It wasn't Elvis, you know. It wasn't Elvis who said that music was the food of love."

"Is that right, Spandau?" says Charlie. "I expect Elvis had other food on his mind. Who was it, then? One of your New Romantic lot?"

"No. It wasn't Elvis, and it wasn't anyone from the New Romantic Wave either, Charlie. It was Shakespeare."

Charlie turns to Lenny. "Clever sod, in' he?"

"Shh, Charlie," comes back Kyrstee with a poke in the back.

"Sorry, Precious. Bit emotional today."

Father Scanlon is in full flow. "Yes, we're here to celebrate one of the great characters of the city of Brighton, Paddy…"

Paddy, what is alive and well and sitting right in front of that daft priest, gives out a little cough.

"Ah, well, so it is," nods Father Scanlon with a smile, "so it is. It's yourself Paddy. And I recognise you just fine I do. Peter, is it? Peter and Paddy, Paddy and Peter. Brothers, twins, and one just as like t'other. Peas in the proverbial pod. Why, tis an easy mistake to make."

Charlie can't resist. "Just a shame it wasn't a bloody double booking!"

"Shh, Charlie!" pokes Kyrstee. "And language! A little respect for the dead, please."

Charlie is working up to full flow. Well, he can't stop himself, can he? "Not that that thieving' little shit ever afforded me any respect."

Brenda, what – as I says – is never happy, is beginning to look a bit nasty now. She's got them daggers in her eyes and you know where they's pointing.

Old Father Scanlon, trooper and that, carries on. He waves his finger at the strange coffin. "Ah yes, Peter Fitzpatrick, tis yourself that's dead and tis yourself that we'll bury. You!" - he points to Paddy - "Well, you'll just have to wait your turn."

The priest shuffles his dementia friendly cards again and goes on. "And, oh yes, for sure, we'll hear some grand tributes. For Peter was a grand fellow, and a good Catholic. And wasn't he not a good businessman too? Three jeweller shops in town! Three!"

Father Scanlon looks up, warming to his theme. "Now, I know, I know, the eye of the needle and all that. But, didn't sweet Jesus himself like a little bit of luxury every now and then? You know, the holy oils, and getting his feet washed and dried nicely by an attractive woman with lovely hair? And can you blame him?"

Some of the congregation is a bit baffled, though it's fair to say that others, you know, them what knows the priest, well, this is just what they was expecting.

"Yes," continues Father Scanlon, "I reckon he was the most successful jeweller in town. Peter, I'm talking about, not Jesus. No, Jesus was more in the carpentry line. But you just try getting a decent carpenter today! And what they'll charge! Sure, haven't I been waiting six months to get the chapel house kitchen cupboards sorted? Yes, we could all do with a little bit of Jesus the carpenter around today. And a fair price he'd charge too. You never heard of Jesus taking anyone to the cleaners!"

This presents another opportunity for a Charlie observation. "Unlike our dear departed friend, Peter bloody Fitzpatrick, who would've shafted his own mother for a bent threepenny bit!"

Them daggers is well sharp now. But, takes more than a bit of heckling to put a professional man of the cloth off his stride.

"But I'm grateful to Peter and Paddy, and to kind… gentle… Brenda, who've err… assured me that they'll have my kitchen sorted right after the funeral."

Back to them dementia friendly cards again. Another quick shuffle.

"Sure, I remember the first time I met them; young lads, Peter and Paddy, Paddy and Peter. Good Catholics, and from the proud county of Sligo." The old priest has a little laugh here, wistful like. Well, he's used to performing from the pulpit. "And sure, weren't they both up on that roof there, just making certain that it was watertight, that the Blessed Virgin didn't suffer with the damp?" He turns to the statue of the virgin in question, and not just for effect, he means it. "Isn't that so, Mary?"

…

Now, let me take you back - if you get my drift - to not long after the arrival of them young Sligo boys in Brighton, some years before they tried their luck and failed in the Big Smoke. There's a young curate, looks a bit like Elvis alright, yeah, just like he was when he did that 1968 TV Comeback Special. Black cassock of course, but also with the leather jacket and greased-back black hair too. He's walking the church grounds. Suddenly he is alerted by a falling slate. He looks up.

"You again! Get your feckin' arses off my roof! You little gobshites! Or so help me, I'll…"

Them Sligo boys come sliding down a drainpipe. "Sorry Father," they says, "we were only looking for birds' nests."

He cuffs them and kicks them, with a fair degree of force too. Well, back then, you was bang to rights keeping feckless youths in order. "Birds' nests?! Birds' nests my feckin' arse!" says he. "You were up to stealing my lead again! I'll give you birds' nests you feckin' little Sligo scumbags…"

The boys wriggle free and hoof it. As they did many times after.

…

Then fast forward to today, and it's like old Father Scanlon's dreaming up a completely different scenario. "Ah yes," he says, "nice lads… And sure, after they made their way in the business world, didn't they just go and pay for a new church roof. Nice boys, good Catholic boys…"

Charlie's not having it. "Bloody Z list felons more like! Out muscled in London by a couple of nutter Kray twins!"

Well, you might say Charlie can talk, given them Fitzpatrick twins just gone and done the exact same thing to him in Brighton.

Old Father Scanlon clocks this observation, well at least the "Ow!" from Charlie what follows another sharp finger in his ribs from his precious Kyrstee. And Brenda heard it clear enough too. It's only a matter of time…

"Now then, now then," says the priest, trying to move things on, "I think we'll start with the tributes, boys. For there's quite a few to get through, and then there's the mass and all… That'll take some time… Now…" He digs deep under all them flashy vestments into a black cassock pocket, "I've a note here from *Graves R Us!*. They say that old Peter might not last too long in the sitting position, so keep them eulogies tight boys. No-one likes a rambler!"

Well, I don't know about that. Some folks is very partial to that daft priest.

Father Scanlon steps down from the pulpit but stops to stare at the strange coffin. "Ah, now, and haven't they done a grand job? But who would have thought that the old rigor mortis would kick in so swift like?" He looks over to Brenda and Paddy. "Though I must say you did him proud, for it was a grand wake."

...

So, let's cast our eyes back once more. No, not to years ago, but to just the night before, in the basement of *Feeney's Bar* in downtown Brighton. General hubbub and what not. There's that daft old priest again, propping up the bar, giving Brenda a rubber ear.

She's trying to clock what Paddy, what is locked in conversation with Charlie, is saying. Something stupid probably. Peter - the dead Peter Fitzpatrick that is - is sitting on a gold painted wooden throne, draped in a purple cape with all sorts of bling round his neck. A china greyhound dog - tribute to his racer, Bundoran Brendan - now also sadly deceased, sits beside him. Don't look nothing like Bundoran Brendan by the way, that mutt statue. But given it is also covered in naff bling, as well as a daft black beanie hat - I mean, what's that about? - well, it's hard to tell who it's meant to be.

Yeah, it's the wake alright, and they's all here: the Fitzpatrick mob and Charlie and his crew too, including Hadley the parrot. It's hard for anyone to hear what anyone else is saying. Well, there's '*Walk like and Egyptian*' blaring from the DJ. Plus, a lot of them old fellas is well Mutt and Geoff.

"Yes," says Paddy to Charlie whilst nodding over at Peter, "said he wanted to take it with him, he did. Just like them old Egyptian pharaohs, you know, buried with their treasure. And we thought - well I did - tis no more than the man deserves. Let's sort out a few things for him to take on his journey from this world into the next."

Charlie gives him a slow and steady polite nod, you know, like when you's only half-listening, and thinking more about what you is about to say yourself.

"So, we had him dressed up as a Egyptian king like, perched on a throne, a bit of nice jewellery, statue of Bundoran Brendan. Yes, all kitted up nice like. And he's taking it all to the grave with him."

Another polite nod from Charlie.

Charlie's old mate Pinkie comes up, and taps his head. "Think I'll hit the road, Charlie. All this noise... Got one of my migraines coming on."

"Yeah, yeah, fair dos," says Charlie. "Always good to see you, Pinkie. We'll catch up after the funeral tomorrow." And off Pinkie goes with a pat on the shoulder from Charlie.

Paddy goes on, well, don't he half... "Wanted to be at his own wake too, like, Peter, insisted! Well, tis his right. 'I want to be sitting up there just like old King Tut,' says he. 'Sitting on a big throne!' And I must say *Graves R Us!* sorted him out very nicely."

Charlie nods, still polite. But he could end up nodding all night here. So, he decides to interject with purpose. "And very good he looks too, Paddy. Very good. You can always rely on *Graves R...* Yes, very regal, very err... Very Ancient Egypt. You must be... proud, pleased, whatever..."

"Oh sure, and Brenda..."

Charlie quickly interrupts. Well, he wants to pull the plug on this polite nodding routine. "And I was thinking myself, Paddy" he says. "What with, you know, what with Peter's passing and that. And then, here's me, you know, not far behind with my prostate cancer. Having to carry around a bag of my own piss..." He gives the bag strapped to his leg a little friendly squelch, just for effect.

"Well, you know, I was thinking, it's time to let bygones be, you know, what they is after all; bygones."

"Absolutely," comes back Paddy, "and that's why you're here, all of you, especially you Charlie Crystal. It was my idea."

"And I do appreciate it, Paddy, we all do." He lays it on a bit thick, does old Charlie. "Lovely wake, lovely. Very, very err… Egyptian." He's trying to get to the point, but with Paddy it takes time.

All of Charlie's old crew - minus Pinkie with the sore head - is sitting round a large table, making best use of the free bar. Trevor, well on the road to happiness, stands up. "That's how they walk," he says, "innit? Them Egyptians?"

Then he does this crappy little Sand Dance thing.

"No, no, here" says Spandau Barry, standing up and depositing his parrot on Bas's shoulder. "Look after Hadley will you, Bas? Careful, he's crapping a bit more tonight. Well, this music is not his sort of thing."

Bas don't look too happy about that.

"Wait a minute," says Trevor bringing out a little blue asthma inhaler and taking a puff.

"You see, it's more like this, Trev," goes on Spandau.

"No, no!" says Trevor.

They's arguing about what hand you lead with, you know, like in them daft old black and white whatshisname Sand Dance films. Wilson, Keppel and what was her name? Betty, was it?

Brenda looks like she's sickening for something, sneering down on everything and everyone from her barstool. Well, she could look down on you from a hole in the ground. Old Father

Scanlon is still rabbiting on, but Brenda is thinking, 'What is that stupid brother of mine saying to Charlie Crystal?!'

"And that is why we have you down as a pallbearer too, Charlie Crystal,'" says Paddy. "You and your chum Lenny will be joining some of the top representatives of the whole of the South Coast operation."

Charlie nods, a little less politely now. "Appreciated, appreciated, Paddy. Distinguished company I do not doubt… But I was thinking, you know… as I was like, you know, two and half years, two and a half <u>long</u> years, banged up in Brixton, as err… a tribute if you will. Taking one for the team as it were. You know, carrying the custodial can, you might say, for, well, not to put too fine a point on it, for yourselves, you and Peter… and whatshername…"

"Sure," says Paddy with a little smirk, "we'd have done the same, Charlie Crystal, if we'd been daft enough to get caught…"

Charlie's mind drifts back to the cold steel of them handcuffs, and the screech of that getaway car; what was sadly also getting away from him.

"Yes, I'm sure but, anyway, my point, Paddy, my point is; whilst I was at Her Maj's displeasure, you and eh, Peter, and… whatshername, proceeded to, well, to be frank, establish a handsome little operation, courtesy of what included my substantial initial capital investment."

"Which we returned to you once you were out."

"To a degree…"

"In full. Allowed you to set up your own little business, did it not?"

Charlie's getting a bit annoyed now. "What?! A poxy little garage, fixin' up knocked-off and Category C motors, and floggin' them off as new?"

"If anyone deserves an interest in fast cars, Charlie, you know, like getaway cars…"

"I shall ignore that. In good grace you might say."

At this point the two of them is nearly knocked over by the rest of Charlie's crew doing that bloody stupid Egyptian Sand Dance.

Charlie is undeterred. "My point is, Paddy, my point is; I emerged into the err… bright light of liberty, to be met with… well, only the gloom of my initial investment. Minus what you might say, was, well, in all fairness, due. You know, collective interest, share of accumulated profits, compound this and that, accrued whatshisnames…"

"It's our operation, Charlie. Not yours. No, we've paid you back, penny for penny, pound for pound, and that's that, Charlie Crystal. We might be villains, but we're not thieves."

…

Got nowhere - didn't he? - Old Charlie.

So, now we's back in the Maculate Concept at the funeral, and one of them villains - not 'thieves' mind - is giving his eulogy, reading from a Brenda script by the sounds of it.

"Yeah, err… lovely man, Peter Fitzpatrick, very honourable. I know I speak for all the err… members of the err… business fraternity: Portsmouth, Poole, Southampton, Hastings, St Leonards err… Newhaven, Folkstone, Ashford. The whole of the err… South Coast operation, err… business network… We's, err, we's all gonna miss Peter, his err… leadership, his drive, enthusiasm, he was a top err… top…"

It's too much for Charlie. Up he gets from his mobility scooter and staggers onto the altar. He's red in the face with effort and anger. "Thief!" he shouts. "Top thief. That's what Peter Fitzpatrick was!"

"Yer," echoes the eulogising villain, "top thief." Then catching himself and Brenda's face, he quickly makes a correction. "No, no, <u>man</u>! Top man! And very <u>honourable</u>."

Father Scanlon can see what's coming. Well, he's been around sinners long enough, and not just in the confessional. "Not just honourable, and a very good Catholic too!" he shouts.

Charlie's having none of it. "Honourable?! Honourable?! He was a bloody thief. And the worst kind; the kind of thief what steals from other thieves! Where's the honour in that?! You tell me!"

Brenda's had it now. She stands up, fuming. "Get off that altar now, Charlie Crystal, or so help me I'll…"

Charlie, well bang in the middle of that altar, now turns to Paddy, looking him straight in the face. "Oh, so it's a woman now. A woman's gonna do your dirty work for you, is it, Paddy Fitzpatrick?! A woman! Here's me crumbling away to nothing, eaten up by a soddin' malignant prostate. A plastic catheter tube rammed right up my todger, and you don't even have the balls to…"

"Get him!" shouts Brenda.

And then, well, what a little fracas ensues. You got Paddy and his villainous company rushing onto the altar and Charlie's supporters doing the same. Well, I say 'rushing', but that is maybe too strong a word. Leastways for some of them. 'Cause, well, there's Lenny and Chen on their mobility scooters, and the rest of the boys from the old crew, well, they is a fair age, as I says. But you got some of their young boys in there too, you know, enjoying a little piece of the action.

Yeah, as I says, it's a tidy little fracas.

In the general melee Charlie takes a mind to rip off his catheter bag and toss it in the general direction of Paddy's mob. Lenny and Chen is driving their scooters over the fighting and thrashing bodies. Old Father Scanlon takes it upon himself to protect the Holy Virgin and stands in front of the Maculate Concept statue. "Ah, now lads," he pleads, "now lads, not the Immaculate Conception, not the Immaculate Conception."

Hadley, the parrot, decides to join in and flies over. He gives it an "Oo-er!" and then drops one on the Blessed Virgin, you know, just as a mark of disrespect. And sure enough, it's by way of a fond farewell too. For despite the parish priest's protests, them scrapping bodies is all over the place and the Virgin Mary topples and smashes to bits.

Ten minutes later, there is the sound of sirens outside.

…

# Chapter 3

So, here we is now, in a bleak room, you'll know what I mean: peeling paint, stains on the floor, dried blood probably, who knows? Maybe even a bit what remains when someone's crapped himself. Yeah, we's down at Brighton's John Street Police Station.

And there's Sergeant Whatshisname, middle-aged miserable git, seen it all before, sitting in front of his little laptop computer. 'Les Misérables', you know, that's what they call him down the station. They say it like 'Lez Misribles'. Yeah, Les Misérables it is, you know on account of his permanent state of miserableness. Well, it's Les for short these days, though his real name's Keith. He's been assigned to interview Charlie, what is sitting across the table, with Kyrstee by his side.

Then there's this junior female police constable - WPC as we used to call them - standing by Sergeant Les. She looks quite kind, tasty too. And to be fair old misery guts has got a bit of smile on his face. No doubt on account of him being more interested in Kyrstee than Charlie. Well, he likes the ladies, does Les. Likes the ladies.

Charlie's doing his best in difficult circumstances. "The thing is Sarg," he says, "the thing is, I was provoked. I was sorely provoked. Otherwise, I mean…"

"Yeah, yeah,' says Les, "we'll get to you in good time, Crystal. All in good time. All in good time. Just let me get a few details down first." He turns to Kyrstee. "So, what's your name?" he asks with a greasy smile.

Kyrstee's smile is a bit more becoming. "Kyrstee."

"Lovely name," says the officer of the law. "Lovely name. And Mrs. Crystal?"

"No, we're err… not married." Still flashing that lovely, clean smile.

Charlie tries to get back into the conversation. "No, we're err… not married. Good as… But you know, given that the third time was not - as they say - lucky. Well, you know, I thought, what chance number four?"

The Sarg continues, talking to Kyrstee that is. "So, you're err… what, in relation to the accused?"

Charlie is naturally indignant. Well, all the best crooks is. "'Ere, I've not been accused of nothing! I'm here out of my own free will!"

As if.

"Yeah," smirks the Sarg, "and courtesy of six police vehicles and thirty officers of the law. Suspected of I don't know what: inciting a riot, actual bodily harm, hate crime in a place of worship for all I know. Desecrating a religious… whatever, by chucking a bag of… hazardous liquid right in the face of a… grieving relative who then subsequently slipped, fell and broke his arm. We'll get to the charges soon enough Crystal, I'm sure…"

This is news to Charlie; good news that is. "I got him then, did I?" he says, looking as happy as a cocker spaniel with his head out a car window. "Pissed on him? After all these years… And he broke his arm too? Double stitching; the silver lining on the silver lining!"

Les takes a deep breath and turns his ingratiating attention back to Kyrstee. "So, where were we, love?"

A little cough comes from that female police constable. "Err, you're not allowed to say that, Sarg."

"Say what?"

"Love."

"Oh, I don't mind," chirps Kyrstee.

"No, she don't mind," confirms Charlie.

"It's not the point," says WPC, "someone else might."

"But I don't."

"No, she don't."

Another sigh, deep and heartfelt, from the Sergeant. "So, err, to return to the point. What is your… err, relationship to the err… to Mr Charles Crystal; notorious small-time villain, thief, crook, fraudster, soft drug peddler, regular jailbird, dodgy second-hand car dealer, with a long list of minor and very irritating offences stretching back over fifty years. A name synonymous with disorganised crime."

Charlie's still trying to join in. "Hey, hey, Sarg, that is unfair. That is totally unfair. D'you know… I mean, think about all them other felons being interviewed at this very moment, right here in them other rooms. They's worse than…"

Les puts him in his place. "If it's a trip down Felony Lane you're after, Crystal, I got a whole dossier in here." He taps his laptop. "With your name writ large all over it. All digital now, but your file, so big, so huge, what with your relentless petty criminal activities, it practically crashed the police central hard-drive!"

There's a pause. Well, there often is after a little speech like that, makes you reflect.

The Sarg comes back; he's not finished. "I mean look at you, Crystal. Look at you! You look like you're just about to pop over to Bognor Butlins for a Lookie-Likie contest. Think you're Michael Caine, do you?! Or is it Charlie Croker?! He's not a real person, you know! The Italian Job?! It's just a film. Yeah, what? Are you're planning a big robbery in Brighton with an escape through the sewers, eh?!" He has a laugh, to himself like, but out loud just the same.

Then there's that pause back again. Well, Charlie's heard that lame gag before, and more than once. 'Maybe I will,' he thinks, 'maybe I will do that very job one day. And stick it right up you.'

But naturally, he don't say this to the Sarg's face.

Kyrstee breaks the uncomfortable silence. "I think it's really good," she says.

"What, err, sorry, lo…" says Les.

"Really good that it's all on your computer. I mean, all that paper saved, all them trees that could've been chopped down, and that's been saved, by you putting all of Charlie's crimes on that little computer."

Another sigh from Les Misérables, though this one with a bit more of a light heart. "I suppose, yes, on the bright side, yes…"

Charlie's still giving it a go. Well, he don't give up so easily, does he? "And I mean, I mean, Sarg. Take a look at some of the err, some of my contemporaries, as it were. What I've had to work with over the years. I mean, the hair-brained schemes what they've come up with… The plans they've presented me with… Bloody ridiculous! I mean, I've said '*No*', so many times. '*No*' I've said." Old Charlie taps his finger hard on the table to make the point. '*No, we're not doin' that. It'll never bloody work!*' I mean my own… minor misdemeanours, indiscretions if you will, over, yes, I accept, a few years, well, these have been more than <u>offset</u> by the crimes what I have personally prevented. You know, by putting a lid on other people's bloody stupid ideas."

Old Les is reduced to a blank stare.

Charlie's not.

"It's like," he goes on, "it's like, you know, your ecology, like your environment, like Kyrstee was saying with your laptop. Like, like you know how them Hollywood Celebs, them A-listers, when they go on holiday, they plant a tree before stepping on their private jet. Don't they? I mean, they offset. Prevent the planet and that. Same thing with me. I mean; by putting a lid on all them stupid ideas, I've offset more criminal activity than I've ever committed myself. Why, I've probably prevented more crime in this town than the whole of the Royal Sussex bloody Constabulary."

"And we're eternally grateful, Crystal. Now, will you shut it?! So, err..." The slimy Sarg turns his attention back to Kyrstee. "So, err... I got a list of alternatives here." He scrolls down screen. "Relationship to the accused... I got 'wife', that's a 'no'. I got 'husband', that's a..." He stops himself, coughs, and turns - despairingly, you might say - to the WPC, and then back to Kyrstee.

"Well, now, I am not assuming nothing, this is after all Brighton; home of the Equality and Diversity brigade..." Another little cough. "And very welcome they are too. But I am not..." - and he looks straight in the eye of his fellow police officer - "not inclined to partake of yet another two weeks compulsory Equality and Diversity training. Wonderful as it was first time round, thank you very much... So, tell me, lo... Ms err... just to be sure, and for the record, am I safe in saying that you are not, Mr Charles Crystal's husband?"

Kyrstee gives one of her little giggles. "I'm not."

"Bloody cheek!" shouts Charlie. "Bloody cheek!"

Old Les is still scrolling. "I got carer?"

"She's not my bloody carer! I don't need no carer!"

"I got... Well, I got a whole list here, to be honest," says the Sarg, "but, rather than go through them all, what would you err... What would you like to suggest?"

"Precious one," says Kyrstee lightly.

"Precious one?"

"Yeah, that's what he calls me, Charlie, his Precious one."

Les is still scrolling down his list of options. "No, no… 'Precious one'… I haven't got that, lo… err…"

Charlie's had enough. "Put down 'partner' for crying out loud! That's what everyone's bloody well called these days."

"Partner, eh?" sniffs the Sarg. "Partner in crime? No, you don't look the sort lo…". Another irritated look at that WPC is followed by his stock greasy smile at Kyrstee again.

"Partner," he types on his laptop, "and next of kin?"

Kyrstee nods.

"N. O. K." says Les as he types. "That's Next of Kin," he winks. "And, let's just get the rest of your err… personal details down proper like. So, err… Kirsty, that's err…" He starts typing and talking again; "K-I…"

"No, it's 'Y'," she interrupts, "Kyrstee with a 'Y'."

"Oh, with a 'Y', eh? K-Y, as in the err… lubricant jelly?"

"Sarg…" says his WPC minder.

"Never thought of that," giggles Kyrstee.

Les starts typing and talking again, like he's back in Primary Three of Middle Street Juniors, you know, reading aloud. "K-Y-R-S-T-Y" he announces with a happy flourish.

"No, there's no 'Y'" says Kyrstee.

"I thought you said there was."

"There's no 'Y' at the end. It's 'double E'."

"Double E?"

"Yeah, K-Y-R-S-T-E-E. Kyrstee!," And the correct spelling is delivered by the owner of that name with another flash of her perfect smile.

"Ohhh… Kyrstee." Les is typing again, got to backspace first. "K-Y-R-S-T-E-E. And very nice too. And your sur…" He looks at WPC, what has got a very serious look on her face. Old Les Misérables hesitates. Well, he's worrying about just about everything he might say now, even a tame little word like 'surname'. 'Cause I mean, like ten minutes of barn-door obvious information packed into two solid weeks of full-time, wall-to-wall, relentless E&D lecturing, well, it's not a lot a fun.

"Second name?" he says.

"Smith," says Kyrstee.

"Smith?"

The nice girl nods.

"Would that be err… 'Smith' with like, I don't know, maybe a silent 'P' at the start?" Les throws a resentful stare at Charlie. "You know, as in Psycho?!"

"No, no," laughs Kyrstee, "just ordinary, S-M-I-T-H."

"Nothing ordinary about you love… err, Ms…err Smith. And what is it you do, err… Ms Smith?"

"I'm an hairdresser, employed. Though I'd love to have my own salon."

"Hairdresser..." Les is still typing and talking. He turns to the WPC. "Has hairdresser got an hyphen?"

"Don't think so, Sarg."

"Now," Les Misérables sits back from his laptop, resting his hands on a comfortable-sized stomach, "if we can just err..." Then he stops, sudden like, sniffs the air with some objection. "What's that... What's that smell? What's.... Is that you, Crystal?" The sarg leans forward over the table squinting at Charlie. "Are you pissing yourself, Crystal?!"

Charlie explains, and with some indignation. "Well, I've lost my bag, haven't I?! Chucked it at that thieving git! What d'you expect? Course I'm leaking. I got a tube hanging out my John Thomas on the road to nowhere!"

Old Les pushes back his chair and stands up with a start. "For Christ's sake. You're disgusting, that's what you are Crystal. Disgusting. Smells like a Kemp Town carsey in here! Get yourself..."

Charlie stands up too, well, let's say, struggles to his feet.

"I'll tell you what it is!" says Charlie. He turns to the WPC, "I'll tell you what it is, love. It's discrimination! That's what it is. I'm a protected species! I've got a catheter! I've got... an assisted mobility vehicle! It's that what d'you m' call it? That thing... It's... undiverse! That's what it is! It's undiverse discrimination!"

"Oh Charlie, you poor thing, "says Kyrstee. And she leans over to help. Unlike them coppers what is taking a good few steps backwards.

Well, understandable, there's a fair old bit of piss splashing about.

...

# Chapter 4

So, now we's in the living room of the flat what sits above Charlie's garage business. And you might observe that there's a bit of a depressed air. Charlie's sitting with his close friends: Lenny, Chen, Spandau Barry with Hadley of course, and there's the old crew too. You know, Bas, Pinkie, Mickey, Coffee-mate, Big Albie, Trevor and a few of their boys as well. A few I say, as most of that younger generation what's come down for the funeral know that there's a better time to be had downtown Brighton than hanging out with a load of old codger villains. So, they's buggered off elsewhere.

There's some big bags of salt and vinegar, and a couple of bottles of Scotch on the coffee table and they's all crunching crisps and sipping whisky from small glasses. A few of them is rubbing the bumps and bruises what they was awarded courtesy of that earlier little Maculate Concept fracas. Still, always a price worth paying, and that little punch-up will live long in perpetuity, it will.

Charlie's giving them the low down on recent events. "Embarrassing, I tell you lads. Embarrassing, that's what it was… And discrimination… For sure, I tell you; I've got a solid case if them charges ever comes to anything."

All the heads nod silently, the crisps is crunched and the whisky is sipped. Well, it's thought provoking, innit?

"I mean," goes on Charlie, "there was this police-bird there also; very nice. Well, quite tasty, but, you know, the right-on type. Anyhows, I thought, at least she'll be sympathetic. But, well, what with my catheter flailing around all over the shop, firing off, you know, in all the wrong directions. I think she might've got some, well… collateral splash, if you get my drift. Maybe that affected her, you know, sensitivities. Anyhows, I got no sympathy, except from Kyrstee."

The heads nod again. The crisps is crunched and the whisky sipped.

"I'll be honest lads, it's not what I'd hoped for, at my time of life - <u>our</u> time of life - I mean… Look at me… Look at <u>us</u>!"

They do; they all look around.

"I mean," says Charlie, "I sort of thought, you know, especially, what with the head of that Clan Fitzpatrick finally popping his clogs. Well… I thought a nice dish of justice might be finally served up. Or at least we'd all get together one more time for a bit of a funereal bash. A celebration of death as old Father Scanlon put it. Rather than spend six hours down the Old Bill only to drown our sorrows over some crisps and a couple of poxy bottles of Scotch!"

They nod, crunch and sip. Well, tastes quite nice actually, that whisky. It's the real McCoy; single malt. Big Albie brought it down special, but now is not the time to correct Charlie.

"And I always thought," goes on Charlie, brimming with reflective sincerity, "you know, that by this time, at this stage in my career, <u>our</u> careers… I mean, I thought that I'd - <u>we'd</u> <u>all</u> - be in a better place. That crime would've somehow paid more handsomely."

"It's not your fault, Charlie," says Bas.

"I feel responsible, Bas. I do."

There's one of them natural pauses. You know, reflective moments.

Trevor helps himself to another handful of crisps. He has a look at the label. "Low fat, low salt?"

"Yeah," says Charlie, "and add onto that low flavour. It's Kyrstee; she's concerned about my heart and kidneys."

"The thing is," says Trevor profoundly, "when you're eating crisps, it's not your heart or kidneys you's concerned about, it's your stomach."

There is murmurs of agreement all round. Well, quite right too. Them crisp manufacturers ought to get a grip.

"D'you know," says Charlie looking over at his old friend Lenny, a little smile flashing across his lips, "I remember when you first moved down here Len, and come along to see me. I thought, here we go, very nice, just what we need in this town; a bit of pace, an injection of fresh blood. You know, I looked at you and I thought he's got the looks, the hair, the style, the build, the movement. I said to myself, yep, we got ourselves a genuine Yardy here. Someone that'll scare the living daylights out of that Fitzpatrick Irish mafia."

They all take a good look at Len and nod. Well, as I says before, he's still in good shape, even if confined to a mobility scooter.

"But then, well," says Charlie, "as soon as you opens your mouth."

Lenny obliges. "What's wrong when I open my mouth then, Charlie?"

Well, you see, Len's got this very strong Birmingham brogue.

Charlie sighs. "The accent, Len, the accent! Don't get me wrong. It has its appeal. A certain..." Charlie shrugs. "You know, charm, friendly, welcoming even. But, in the world of crime... Well, there's like, there's certain accents what tick all the boxes. A hierarchy of threat, you might say. Voices what simmer with malevolence, if you get my drift. Like your South Londoners, your Cockneys, your Glaswegians, Geordies even. But your Brummie, well, I don't know what it is, but it just, it just don't cut it."

Poor Lenny looks indignant, well as much as someone from the West Midlands can.

Charlie then turns his attention to Chen. He's in some sort of groove now. "And then when you's turned up Chen, my hopes was raised again."

"What's wrong with a Scouser then?!" says Chen, a little bit peeved, you might say.

"Not a lot," replies Charlie. "Not a lot. Plenty of crime up in Liverpool. A city with commendable criminal credentials."

Everyone nods. Well, it's true.

"And?" says Chen.

Charlie shrugs again. "Well, Chen. You know, when I saw you, I was hoping for someone with, you know, maybe a few international links. Like we'd be as tight as a Triad. You know, something a bit more exotic than South Toxteth."

Lenny feels the need to complain, and with good cause, you might say. "Charlie, this is all beginning to sound a bit racist."

"Yeah, Charlie," says Chen.

"Racist? Me? No! No, it's not!" says Charlie. "I'm just lamenting the fact that you's not more… effective criminals. What's wrong with that?"

"More like that we're not foreign enough!" says Chen. "My family's been in Liverpool for three generations!"

"Is that right? Doing what, Chen?" asks Spandau, a whiff of interest in his voice. You know, trying to inject a little bit of social conversation into the mix.

"Well," says Chen, and he breathes in and out deep like, "laundry mainly…"

"Laundry?!" shouts Charlie. "Chinese bloody laundry?! And you're calling me racist?!"

And there's another bit of uncomfortable pause what follows.

Then Chen - well, it's like he's almost talking to himself now - starts up quietly. "Yeah, it was always laundry. I suppose I broke the mould, you know, moving into crime. My daughter… Well, you could say she's still involved in, well, like the cleanliness business; works for the Environmental Health down the Council. But I like to think like she's still, you know, a bit corrupt; a chip off the old block."

"Well," says Len, also getting back in the swing of things, "everyone's corrupt down the Council, Chen. Political organisation. I mean, if you can't trust your politicians to be corrupt, who can you?"

Just at this moment, young Reg walks in and interrupts the conversational flow. Bit of a spring in his step, has Reg. He knows most of them sitting round the table. Well, maybe not the latest generation so much, but certainly Lenny, Chen and Spandau. And Charlie's old mates has been down regular enough.

"Come in, Reg," says Charlie, "come in. You know the boys, and you remember Bas, Pinkie, Mickey, Coffee-mate, Big Albie, Trevor. And they's brought some of their lads too."

There's a lot more nodding, crunching and sipping.

"I just about got that Range Rover sorted, Charlie, you know, the Evoque," says Reg. "Come up nice. Looking very tidy."

"Thank you, Reg," is Charlie's reply. "We'll get a good price for that. Got some interest from err… Africa, as a matter of fact."

Reg casts an eye round the room. "You all right for drinks?"

"Yeah, all good, thanks, Reg," says Charlie, and with a nod over his shoulder adds, "she's in there." And then it's like he suddenly clocks something. "'Ere, 'ere," says Charlie to them round the table. "None of you lot is on them anticoagulants or nothing, is you? I mean this stuff" - he holds up his empty glass - "well, it don't mix well with some medications."

There's considerable shaking of heads, but the question prompts a brief and revealing discussion.

"I got these, err… Triptan patches," says Pinkie. "You know." He gives his head a tap. "But don't do nothing for them headaches, really. Nothing…"

Then Big Albie pipes up. "I got the right hip done a couple a years back. And now the left's got a bit dodgy, but all they give me is paracetamol."

Coffee-mate's turn. "I got Atrial Fibrillation." He holds up this tiny small box of medication. "But I can't take them blood thinners. *'Aspirin'* they said. I said *'Aspirin? My mum give me that as a kid.'* Then they says, *'Oh you can't give kids aspirin no more. It's dangerous.'*"

Everyone looks surprised. Well, naturally. I mean, what's wrong with a couple of aspirin all of a sudden?

"I had that fibrination once," says Bas, "but they said I don't need no medication, however if it come back…"

"I got a ton of inhalers in here," interrupts Trevor. Well, he would have, wouldn't he? Then he goes and pulls out all these multi-coloured puffers and the like, what then spill all over the floor. "All useless," he says. "I mean, first they said it was asthma, now they's saying it's COPD, whatever that is…"

Charlie's had enough. "Yeah, alright, alright! We's all got something! Why there's Lenny, Chen and me having to travel round town on toy tricycles, with a big '*Look at me, I'm Disabled*' sticker plastered all over our foreheads." He turns to Pinkie. "You Pinkie; you should see old Doc Walker for them headaches. Walker, Doctor Marten Walker. Marten with an 'e'."

"What, like Kyrstee?" says Spandau.

Charlie gives him one of his looks, not quite in the same league as Brenda Fitzpatrick, but it does the job. "Same for you, Albie," he goes on, "I mean if you're in pain. Like, over the years I've helped old Doc Walker with err… well, some supplies of what is not, well, readily available on prescription. You know, for his personal usage and such. And in return he's always looked after me good and proper."

"Not stopping you from dying though, is he Charlie?" observers Lenny.

That one halts Charlie right in his tracks. "No," he says. "No."

And would you Adam and Eve it? There's another one of them uncomfortable pauses. This is supposed to be a friendly gathering of old mates, for crying out loud!

"Well," says Reg, with a cough and a nod to the door. "I'll just err…"

"Yeah, yeah, of course, thanks Reg," says Charlie. Then he winks. "Oh, and err… Make it a bit special tonight, Reg, if you don't mind. I mean, she's had a hard day, and been very err… you know, understanding."

Reg quietly opens a door and disappears into another room.

"You know, it's funny, innit," says Spandau, "Fitzpatrick, taking it all with him, or some of it like. You know, like them old Egyptian Pharaohs?"

"Madness," says Len.

"What a waste," says Chen.

"I mean, imagine," continues Spandau, expanding his little theme, "imagine if there was like a tomb raider, you know, like in the old days. And Fitzpatrick was sitting in a tomb, instead of like six feet under. I mean, someone'd just come along and nick the lot, wouldn't they?"

Charlie perks up. "Say that again, Spandau."

"Say what?"

"What you was just saying."

"I was just saying, you know, if we were in ancient Egypt, chances are, some tomb robber, grave robber, whatever, would come along and nick all that jewellery that's been buried with him."

"Yeah..." says Charlie, nodding in thoughtful agreement. "They would, and they'd be quite right too... You know, I reckon that Fitzpatrick's been buried with enough... to cover, you know, well, to cover some - a sizeable proportion if you will - of what is due me... due us all!"

"And?" says Len. "What are you getting at Charlie?"

"And we could take it."

"What? Rob his grave?" says Chen.

"Recover what is rightly ours," corrects Charlie.

"Dig him up?" says Chen.

"Yeah."

"And nick all his buried treasure?"

"Chen, my friend, I couldn't have put it more concisely myself." Charlie suddenly has a rather satisfied smile, like he's already gone and done the job.

Now, at this point, all of them sitting around the table, nodding heads, crunching crisps and sipping whisky - apart from Charlie it would seem - becomes aware of certain noises of pleasure what is coming from the adjacent room. Of course, it's Reg and Kyrstee making a night of it. Well, you know how it is when you's in a room and you hear noises of intimacy coming through the wall, especially when you know the parties involved. It's well... It's uncomfortable.

"'One for the road' you might say," continues Charlie well into his stride. "One last little corn on the cob. We all go along tomorrow evening, take a little digger along with us. I mean, you could source that at short notice, Spandau?"

"Certainly," says the old New Romantic.

"Ground'll be nice and soft," says Charlie. "We dig, take what is ours, I mean, I'm not interested in any desecration or nothing. Well, I might throw in a bit of piss, but that'd be it. No. We remove the spoils of war, fill the hole back in. It'll be like no-one'll even know we's been there."

Lenny is not convinced. "Charlie, if they <u>have</u> buried old Fitzpatrick with all that bling…"

"What, d'you think they was just making it up then, Len?"

Lenny shrugs.

"Well, I mean Len," says Charlie with a big grin. "There's only one way to find out!"

"But Charlie," insists Len, with reasonable forethought, you might say, "if they have buried him with any gold, they they're gonna have guards all around that grave."

"What? No, they're too cocky. They'll think no-one would ever dare."

Them noises off - the sexual ones that is - well, they's getting louder and louder. Even that parrot's noticed.

"Oo-err…" squawks Hadley, in his Brummie accent. Well, I expect he's picked that up from old Spandau Barry himself.

"Not now, Hadley," says the old New Romantic.

"No," goes on Charlie. "Them Fitzpatricks'll never even think of it. We only just did, and that was by accident, 'cause Spandau here was going on about them ancient Egyptians."

Them sex noises is now reaching the ecstasy stage. Charlie's mates is obviously embarrassed, though them young lads is all smiling, seem to be enjoying it. Must be a generation thing that.

"Saucy!" says Hadley.

Where'd he learn them words, that parrot?

And I mean, all the time Charlie's acting like nothing's happening. "What d'you say lads?" he says. "Interested in extending your stay in the fair city of Brighton for another night?"

There's a barrel load of 'Oohs' and 'Ahhs' what comes from that bedroom and it seems like the behind doors proceedings has come to a close. But Reg and Kyrstee is young folks. You know what that means. It's only a matter of time, minutes probably, before it all starts up again.

Bas stands up, he's had enough and he don't want to hang around for any encore. He gives his throat a little clear. "I think err... I think I'll err... call it a night, Charlie. You know, get back to the old Premier Inn. Hit the sack. I'd love to come along tomorrow but err... the missus, well, she's got early dementia you know, and, well, can't leave her on her own too long. I'd be very happy to look at, you know, something later, if you've got anything else, a more detailed... You know, plan like..."

Pinkie follows his example. "Yeah, me too, Charlie, be very interested, but err... better head off now. Got a err... big day tomorrow, what with err... you know..."

Big Albie's just the same. "Yeah, me too, Charlie."

One by one - or rather all together and pretty sharpish for a bunch of old geezers - all of Charlie's friends and their relevant offspring, except of course Spandau Barry, Lenny and Chen, take their leave.

Charlie looks at the remainder. "So, it's me. You, Len?" Lenny nods. "Chen?" He does the same. "And Spandau?" A final nod.

Well, there's been a lot of nodding, crunching and sipping this evening, but I think that will call matters to a close.

Oh wait, here's Trevor come back up the stairs. He's forgotten his cap.

"Yeah, sorry, I need to get back to Reading, Charlie," he says. "Got a visit from the grandkids tomorrow, otherwise... you know... Sounds like a great scheme, though. I mean, what could possibly go wrong?"

...

## Chapter 5

Well, this.

There is a bright moon in a dark sky. And the stars? Well, they do look lovely. For we is no longer in town, so the light pollution don't interfere so much, see. Still, that is of little or no consequence given as we's in a graveyard on top of a steep hill. So, it is not a place where the occupants - six feet under as they all is - have much scope for star gazing.

And fresh in his grave, Peter Fitzpatrick's has a nice mound of earth - well, that was a fair-sized coffin - indicating to anyone what might be interested, where he lies resting in an early state of peace. A suitable tasteless headstone will no doubt be erected once the ground has settled.

A somewhat stately - if you will - procession of Charlie, Lenny and Chen arrive on their virtually silent mobility scooters slowly crossing the grass what grows over the deceased. Sort of respectful in a way. Spandau Barry follows them in a small noisy digger, bright orange, not so discrete, and neither so respectful you might say.

Them scooters then all line up on one side of the Fitzpatrick grave with their headlights shining on it, and Spandau Barry with his digger goes 'round the other.

Charlie gives the nod, but just as that digger is about to come to life and pierce the earth, bright floodlights come on all around and illuminate the scene. And there stands Brenda with Paddy beside her. He's got his right arm in plaster and in a sling. They is not alone. No, there's several other threatening hoodlums dotting the hillside all around.

"I was expecting you," says Brenda quietly. "Hoping actually. You know, what with your… little performance at my brother's funeral."

Charlie's upset. Well, you would be, wouldn't you?

"He should never have said that!" he shouts. "He should never have said that!"

"Who? Said what?" says Len.

"Trevor! That! *'What could possibly go wrong?'* he says. It's like, it's like one of them cheap clichés, you know, just asking for it. One minute you got your crook's naïve certainty, and the next... Well, it's all gone piss pear-shaped! It's the kiss of bloody death, that's what it is. He should never've said it!"

"Maybe more like one of them old Egyptian curses, you know, on tomb raiders, Charlie?" suggests Spandau Barry.

Charlie shakes his head and points his finger in the air. "The next time I see Trevor..."

Brenda steps forward. "So, you were warned, in your own daft way... And yet still..."

Charlie tries to recover his composure. "Brenda, we's just come to pay our respects."

"Respects?" asks Paddy.

Well, takes everything literally, that man-boy.

"Yeah," says Charlie, "pay your brother the respects what he deserves."

"You don't half make some cock-eyed decisions, don't you Charlie Crystal?" says Brenda.

Charlie looks straight at Paddy. "So, this is it? Is it? She's in charge now, is she? Brenda?"

That annoys both of them Fitzpatricks, though not quite in the same way.

"What is it with you and women?" says Brenda, her voice getting a bit edgy now.

"I don't know what you mean," says Charlie, all innocent like.

"I mean you're a misogynist, aren't you? You hate women."

"Me?" says Charlie, genuinely puzzled. "Why, I've been married three times, might as well call it four. I love women."

"You love women?" Brenda comes down to stand next to him, limping a bit, well that cheese and onion's not been sorted yet. She leans on Charlie's mobility scooter. "I don't think so. You can't bear the idea of a woman being in control, being in charge."

"I don't know what you're talking about!" says an affronted Charlie. "I, I cut my criminal teeth in 60s when you women was all wanting to wear them mini-skirts with your long legs out and that. And I said, *'Good on you girls, good on you!'* I was all for it.

And then, then, in the 70s when you was all burning your bras, I fanned the flames didn't I? I fanned the flames. I said, *'Yeah, you go girls! Get them off and get them out!'*

And then, and then, in the… in the 80s and 90s, when you's changed your tune again, and it was all like your push-up bras and *'Hello Boys! Cop a load o' this!'* I took a good look, didn't I? Well, be rude not to!"

There's very few people what does a withering look of contempt better than Brenda Fitzpatrick, not even Les Misérables, and that is exactly what she does.

"I'll admit,' carries on Charlie, "I'll admit that the err… 21st century, what with your lesbians and other err… GBTs… and err…

pluses and things, well… it's been… a bit more complicated. But I've had old Spandau Barry here," - he gives him a nod - "as a gay man, you know, to keep me on the… help me err… navigate the err… bent and broad, if you will. And of course, I <u>have</u> been in prison! Well, you meet all sorts in there!"

Brenda says nothing, well, she don't have to.

"But my point is," says Charlie, "my point is; whether you's been wanting your skirts long or short, your legs in or out, your bras on or off, or your tits up or down, I mean, I've been very supportive! I'm a ladies' man!"

Brenda looks him right in the eye. "You just don't get it, Charlie Crystal, do you? You - just - don't - get it."

Charlie's still all innocent, genuine like. "I don't know what you <u>mean</u>."

And he don't.

Brenda takes a look around. "You <u>do</u> know how this little scene ends though, don't you?"

She gives the signal to her hoodlums who then promptly eject Charlie, Lenny and Chen from their scooters, and chuck Spandau Barry off the digger. Then one of them villains climbs up onto that same digger.

Charlie's a bit more hesitant now. "Yeah," he says, "I am familiar with… I have err… witnessed this sort of situation before… in the err… in the cinema as a matter of fact."

Well, we all know what's coming. We's all seen the same film.

The villain operating the digger, lifts up Charlie's scooter and throws it down the hill.

"Nice scooter," says Brenda.

Charlie gives a nonchalant shrug. "I will require those err… plates back. Went to a lot trouble acquiring them in the first place."

Brenda gives the nod again, and Lenny's and then Chen's scooters suffer the same fate.

Charlie's trying to talk things up, not exactly from a position of strength, you might say. "You ought to be more careful, you know," he says. "You know what could happen next in a scenario like this, don't you?"

"I'll take my chances," says Brenda. "Anyway, word is you've only got a few weeks left before you join big brother Peter here six feet under. If that wasn't the case, I might be inclined to take more drastic action. But I understand that a very - very - painful natural death awaits you, and I wouldn't want to deprive you of that now, would I? You don't have any children, do you, Charlie Crystal?"

That puts Charlie on the spot. "No, well err… Well, not that I'm aware of…"

"So, it's just you, then," says Brenda. "The end of the Crystal line… Of course, we've got Paddy's boy, young Paddy to carry on our business."

Paddy and young Paddy, really? I mean, put the two of them together and it still wouldn't to add up to a three figure IQ.

"Well," says Charlie, well aware of this fact, "that must be a great err… comfort to you."

"Comfort enough," says Brenda. "Comfort enough."

Well, it's true; that is all she got, has Brenda. Never had no kids of her own like, see. Not sure if she even ever, well, you know… I mean, well, she's the sort of creature what would devour her mate after copulation. So, I mean… if she did ever, you know, well, probably no witnesses left alive to testify.

Brenda decides it's time to sign off things. She turns her back on Charlie. "Well, it's time to go."

"'Ere!" says Charlie. "How's we supposed to get back to Brighton, then?"

"Oh, we've thought of that," says Brenda.

She gives the eye to a couple of them villains who then chuck three walking frames in front of those unfortunates what has been recently dispossessed of their mobility scooters.

"Very funny…" says Charlie.

"Oh, and take away their phones, lads" adds Brenda as she walks off, " and Spandau Barry's car keys and that digger too. Wouldn't want them cheating by getting a lift or phoning for an Uber now, would we?"

The phones and keys is duly removed, and off drives a villain in that noisy digger.

"Oh, and err…" says Paddy, desperate to get in on the act. "Brighton's that…" he tries to lift his broken arm to point in the correct direction, but puts it down in pain. "That way…" he says, pointing awkwardly across his body with his good arm.

The headlights go out and Charlie and company is left looking up at the stars, even if, at one with all them deceased underground, they's hardly in the best position to enjoy the night sky.

…

And it is some three hours later that a very old looking Charlie Crystal shuffles into his first floor flat above the garage gripping a walking frame. He's got Spandau's New Romantic cloak wrapped round him, though he looks more like an old woman than an 1980s heart-throb pop star.

Yeah, I mean, here we is, not long arrived in the 21$^{st}$ century and old Charlie looks like he's just wandered in from the 19$^{th}$. Michael Caine look-a-like? I don't think so. More like Old Mother Riley.

He falls with a dull thud on the floor and the Zimmer makes a sort of jangling noise what awakens Kyrstee.

There she is at her bedroom door, in her nightdress.

"Charlie! Charlie!" she says, when she sees him. "Look at you!"

She runs in and helps Charlie onto the sofa. She's got a nice touch, has Kyrstee. Gentle like.

Charlie lies there, exhausted. He has a good cough and then winces. That cough helped, and well, at the same time it didn't help neither. He's obviously in severe pain.

"What happened?" says Kyrstee.

"You don't wanna know, Precious," he says. "You don't wanna know…"

Kyrstee's now kneeling down on the carpet beside Charlie and she starts caressing his hair.

"Oh Charlie…" she whispers.

And then poor old Charlie gives out a loud groan. I tell you it sounds awful. It's like a howl from beyond the grave. He's feeling is age and his condition, for sure.

That noise panics Kyrstee. Well, she's never really seen Charlie like this. She shouts out, "Reg! Reg! Come in here!"

And sure enough, there's young Reg in his boxer shorts, come running out the bedroom.

...

## Chapter 6

Charlie's lying on a couch, only it's a different one now. It's the examination couch of old Doc Walker; Dr Marten Walker - Marten with an 'e' - Charlie's GP.

He's a tall, well-built fellow, Doc Walker, even if he has passed the sixty ticket. Deep, strong, clear Scottish voice too; sort of trustworthy authority, you know. Like they used to always say Scottish doctors is the best. Yeah, bit like Scottish bank managers. That is 'til all that Royal Bank of Scotland shenanigans. Mind you, the old doc's been up to a few tricks of his own over the years. Yeah, a bit like them Scottish bank managers…

Anyhows, here he is, washing his hands having just completed his examination of a very particular patient.

"Well, it was very good of you to see me, doc," says Charlie, still on the couch.

"Always a pleasure, Charles."

"'Specially with them doctors' appointments so hard to come by."

"Hmm…"

I tell you; it's like a rumble from the deep when he does that, old Doc Walker.

Charlie does his imitation of the practice's phone answering service. "'You are 35$^{th}$ in the queue'. Remember you can always bugger off somewhere else and get the same NHS welcome. Then that bloody muzak torturing you…"

"Hmm…" That rumble again. "Well, I know how you feel, Charles. Personally, I'd like to retire but we're so short, I just can't leave."

"Very noble, doc. Very noble. Difficult times for the old NHS."

"And what with the time I had off practice, with, you know, various... issues... Well, my pension doesn't look quite as healthy as it might."

"Sorry to hear that doc. But, you know, maybe we could err... like, you know, come to some arrangement, to err... What is it? Boost your lump sum?"

"Very kind, Charlies," says the doctor like he's listening when he's not really. Well, he's had a whole medical career to perfect that one.

The doc sits down and scribbles on a note of paper, then gets up and hands it to Charlie. "This is my new mobile number. You're *End of Life Care* now, Charles. No more hour-long telephone queues."

"Thank you, doc," says Charlie scrumpling up the paper into his pocket. He's still lying there on the examination couch by the way.

Doc Walker starts typing on his computer. "These painkillers will give you powerful pain relief, Charles. Slip them under your tongue and they'll act in minutes. And I'm going to give you my own special combo; steroids with a wee bit of methylphenidate on the side. It'll perk you up; give you some energy, more appetite, some zip, and a bit more concentration too for these last few weeks."

Charlie nods. "Appreciated. Appreciated, doc."

"Mind" continues the doctor, "you haven't done yourself any favours with a three-mile hike in the middle of the night. What were you thinking? You've got secondaries up and down your spine. It could just collapse. And you've got another one pressing on your aorta. That's your main artery, Charles. It could pop any moment."

"Well, let's hope it holds off a bit longer," says Charlie. "'Cause I got a little score to settle."

"Those Fitzpatricks, eh? Never liked them myself," says the doc. "Stitched me up more than once, you know, grassed me up to the GMC among other things, just because I wouldn't play ball… Well, there's villains and there's villains."

"There is, doc, there is, and me - and to a certain extent - your good self, well, we fall into the first category."

The doc gives a sort of humph laugh and then one of his deep, deep rumbles.

Then there's a natural pause. Well, I know, there's a few in this story, but that's life. We don't all go about talking over each over all the time.

"You've been very unlucky, Charles," continues the doc. "Most men either get a large prostate that stops them pissing straight, or a small cancerous one that quickly spreads and takes them to the grave. You got both."

"Blessed, eh, doc?"

That natural pause pops up again. It's the right moment for the doc to ask that intimate question.

"So, Charles," says the good doctor, "how d'you feel about dying?"

"Well…" and Charlie has a think. "I can't say I'm over the moon about it, doc, but to be honest, I thought I'd go sooner."

"Hmm." Another rumble. An encouraging one, you know, to talk more.

And Charlie does. "I mean, death, don't get me wrong doc, it is a loss, and no-one'll feel it more than me. But I tell you…" And there's a little bit of emotion creeping into Charlie's voice now. "Living too long," he says, "living too long, doc… That is an even greater loss."

Charlie sits up and swings round on the examination couch, taking a deep sigh.

"I don't want to be remembered as some disabled, declining, faltering old git. You know, feeble, pathetic, literally can't piss on his own."

The doc nods in agreement. "How did you get here today?"

"Kyrstee." Charlie eyes the door. "She's outside. Had to come in the car, didn't I? Reg is sorting out some new mobility vehicles for us, so Kyrstee's doing her chauffeur bit. But I don't want her in here. She's not my carer!"

"No… But you are at a stage where you do need looking after."

Another pause. Both men is thoughtful, now. The doc is still waiting for Charlie to speak up, you know, open up a bit more. He knows his craft, does Doc Walker. And Charlie does cut loose.

"You know, doc," he says, "I always thought my final furlong would be a bit more dramatic. You know what I mean? And I really believed I'd be further ahead of the field.

In my quieter moments, I sometimes speculated, you know, that I'd be gunned down by an army of specialist firearm officers whilst making off with some gold bullion. Or maybe crushed in a dramatic car chase across some of the more scenic parts of London. You know, following a nice little bank heist. Or at least bludgeoned into oblivion by a jealous husband as I was tuckin' into his delicious missus... But..." And Charlie takes another deep sigh. "All that's beyond me now."

Rumble, rumble. Well, it's therapeutic in these circumstances.

"I was wondering, you know, doc," goes on Charlie, "and err..." He has a little clear of his throat. "This might help with your pension pot too... if you might be inclined to, you know, help out a bit, when err... Well, when push comes to shove. Maybe..." Charlie shrugs. "Maybe ease my passage from here into the next err... eternal here-ever-after... I don't wanna be, you know..."

"I see," says the doc.

"I mean," goes on Charlie, "state of things as they is now, you know, like as not in a few years... Well, it'll be compulsory for geezers like me..."

"Hmm," rumbles the doc.

"It's just a matter of time." Another shrug from Charlie.

And another rumble from the old doc. I mean, could mean anything, that rumble.

"And you agree?" asks Charlie, a note of optimism in his voice.

The doc clears his throat. "Put it like this, Charles. You and I have always enjoyed a certain... understanding; a doctor-patient relationship like no other, you might say."

"In a good sense, I hope."

"Oh, in so many senses. My own err... dalliances if you will, have often relied, to some degree on your discreet and err... accommodating nature. Anyway, without wishing to revisit all, what the err... General Medical Council has err... before, you know, summed up so comprehensively..."

"Absolutely," says Charlie brightly.

Well, it's his turn to encourage the doc to speak up, innit?

"I feel... Well, let me put it like this," says the doc. "We share a common enemy, and as long as you and I can maintain a mutually... therapeutic relationship. Well... I'm here to help."

Charlie stands up, hobbles over to the patient's chair and pats the doc's shoulder before sitting down. "Thank you, doc, thank you," he says. "Would we err... need to clear anything with anyone, you know like them undertakers? That's how they got Old Shipman, weren't it? Suspicious undertakers."

"Well, I'm no Shipman..."

"No but... Them *Graves 'R' Us!*; they's in the pockets of the Fitzpatricks."

"Yes." agrees the doc. "You'd be better with *Deepe and Stiff*. They don't have a lot of time for the Fitzpatricks either, and they'll always happily accept a bung."

Charlie nods. "*Deepe and Stiff*, of course. Name on the tin and all that."

Rumble, rumble.

"Well, doc, you're a Godsend,' says Charlie. "No doubt about it."

Charlie struggles to his feet, gripping the pain in his stomach and back. The doc stands up to help him, and he does steady up. Then, to seal the deal, they shake hands.

As the doc opens the door for Charlie, he turns to him. Some final words of advice.

"Just you take good care of yourself, Charles Crystal. I know about your determination to win as you head down the home straight, even if it is just by a nose… But all I'm saying is, be careful. Don't do anything rash."

"Oh, don't you worry doc," says Charlie smiling. "Whatever I do will be well thought through… very considered. You can bet your doctor's licence on it."

Rumble, rumble. "You'll forgive me if I don't."

And out toddles old Charlie, a weight off his shoulders.

If only every doctor was so accommodating.

…

# Chapter 7

We's back inside Charlie's flat above the garage. He's got a bit more colour about his cheeks, and a bit more vitality, you know; pep. Well, probably them medicines what the good doc gave him. Given him a lift and what not.

He's sitting with his close buddies; Lenny, Chen and Spandau Barry complete with the ever-present Hadley. No whisky this time. Just mugs of tea on the table. You see, it's a planning meeting. Clear heads is called for.

Chen's in one of his nutty moods. I don't know where they come from. "You know," he says idly into the thoughtful silence, "I've never really understood the difference between Brainstorming and Blue-Sky Thinking."

"This is err... as I say, Brainstorming, Chen," says Charlie flatly.

Such conversational gambits always pique old Spandau's interest. "I see, Charlie," he says, "so, we should consider the practical constraints on any of our err... creative ideas?"

"Sorry?" says Charlie.

"Well," continues Spandau, "with Blue-Sky Thinking, Charlie, ideas need not be grounded in reality."

Lenny's puzzled. "Well, we want to stay in reality, Barry. We don't want to be out there like we've just swallowed a plate of magic mushrooms."

"I've never tried them, you know," says Chen. "They're on my bucket list."

Spandau won't have his intellectual flow disrupted. He continues. "But on the downside, by Brainstorming, we remain inhibited by current constraints, and run the risk of discarding an idea, simply because of obstacles that, while relevant in the here and now, may in the future become obsolete."

"What?" says Charlie, immediately wishing he hadn't asked.

"For example," goes on Spandau, "you might not have conceived of a plan for Internet Fraud in the 1980s, because the Internet had not been invented. Well, not properly anyway."

"Eh?" says Charlie.

"But Barry," says Len, "what would be the point of planning an Internet fraud if the Internet wasn't invented?"

Chen's pleased with himself. He can solve that one. "Ah!" he says, "Well, you'd be first off the mark when it was!"

Charlie, he's got that look, you know, confusion and annoyance. It's a look he's had many times in this company.

"What I'm saying…" says Spandau with emphasis, "is…"

"Stop! Stop! Stop this!" shouts Charlie. "What am I working with here? You is all supposed to be criminally intelligent. What, was all them years in prison wasted on you? Didn't you pick up nothing?"

"I picked up Herpes once…" says Spandau dolefully. "Well, you never really get rid of it, lies dormant and…"

"Stop it!" shouts Charlie again. "All I'm looking for is a few good ideas!!! Bloody hell."

They proceed once more in solemn silence, what after less than a minute is broken by Lenny who sums up the facts as they is known.

"You want to rob all the Fitzpatrick jewellers?"

Charlie nods. "Correct."

"And get clean away with it?"

"Naturally."

"And not <u>even</u> be suspected of having done it?"

"That is the err… general idea, Len."

"But Charlie," observes Spandau - with some acuteness, you might say - "if the Fitzpatricks are done over, you'll be first on the list of suspects. The Old Bill, or worse the Fitzpatricks, will sweep you up before you can say Jack bloody Robinson."

"True," says Charlie, nodding. "True. And that particular Jack and me, well… We is already very well acquainted."

"Oh," says Chen with a note of surprise. "Did you know a Jack Robinson as well then, Charlie? I went to school with one, you know like. Nice lad. Terrible stammer. Took him an age just to say his own name."

Charlie stares at Chen, his mouth open in wonderment. "Is it… I mean, sometimes… I wonder Chen. It is me? Or is it…"

"Look Charlie," says Spandau bringing him back to the here and now. "You hate the Fitzpatricks and they hate you. For crying out loud their attempted rapprochement ended with you chucking a bag of piss all over them at a funeral!"

"And the thought of it still gives me great pleasure, Spandau."

"What's a rapprochement?" asks Lenny.

"I think it's like a ramp," says Chen.

"No, it's a..." says Spandau but Chen interrupts, having already explained it. "It's true Charlie," he says. "Everyone would know it was you."

"The only way you'd get away with it, Charlie," says Spandau, "would be if you were already dead... But that's Blue Sky Thinking."

"What d'you mean?" says Chen. "Like a zombie robbery?"

"Leave it, Chen," says Lenny, clocking that look in Charlie's eyes. "Blue Sky, as Barry says. Not required."

"No, no," insists Chen. "There's lots of examples of zombies doing all sorts. I mean I've seen..."

"Yeah, in the films, Chen," says Spandau. "In films."

"But what starts in the cinema... Life imitating art... Pre-Internet and all that..." says Chen, wagging his head like a nutter.

Charlie's now got his own head in his hands, when Reg walks in and they all look up.

"Hello fellas," says Reg, bright as a button, as ever. "All good?"

There is the usual nods and murmurs of acknowledgement, but some nervousness too from Charlie's mates. Well, they know what's coming.

"Saucy!" squawks Hadley. And they haven't even started yet.

"Well," says Reg smiling. "I got three nice mobility vehicles lined up down there for you all, as replacements, Couldn't get much from the previous - scrap really - but we got the plates back. Shouldn't be long, now."

He looks at Charlie's company. "And Charlie's suggested another three separate vehicles, extra re-enforced jobs, a real bit of oomph." He turns to Charlie. "That'll take a bit of time, Charlie, but I think I'll get there."

Charlie's pleased, at least someone's got a bit of sense. "Excellent, Reg. Excellent. I'm sure I'll find good use for them," he says.

"Yeah, that's great, Reg," says Chen.

"Yeah, thanks very much, Reg," says Len.

"You lot all right for transport tonight?" asks Reg.

"Yeah, yeah," says Len hurriedly. "Barry's err… giving us a lift."

"Very nice." Reg turns his attention to Spandau Barry. "You still driving that…"

"Yeah…" nods Spandau.

"If you ever wants a trade-in, you know, I'm sure we could sort something…"

"Yeah, very kind, thank you… Reg."

That uncomfortable pause what was just waiting round the corner, duly arrives.

"Well, I'll just err…" says Reg, nodding in direction of bedroom door.

Chen coughs, "Yeah, err… Good night, Reg."

"Yeah. Good night, Reg," says Len and Spandau together.

So, Reg exits 'stage left', closing the door quietly behind him, and after a few seconds Lenny struggles to his feet.

"Well, I think we best be heading, Charlie."

"What? No, hold on, just a minute." Charlie looks surprised.

There's that first squeal of excited laughter from behind the bedroom door. Chen, Lenny and Spandau exchange some anxious glances.

That saucy parrot's been waiting for it. "Oo-err…" squawks Hadley.

Spandau clears his throat and says, "I was wondering, Charlie, maybe it's best, you know… if we don't meet here."

"Yeah, I was thinking the same," says Lenny.

"Yeah, it might be easier if err…" mumbles Chen.

"More convenient…" says Len, and they all nod.

"We could, you know," says Spandau, "use the upstairs at *The Duke*. They hate the Fitzpatricks as much as us, so they're pretty tight, and they got a stair lift there now…"

Charlie is however, you know, like waking up from one of them thoughtful reveries.

"What d'you mean?" he says. "I've got a bloody stair lift here! And I hate the Fitzpatricks more than anyone! What's wrong with here? We'd have to pay for *The Duke*."

Well, exactly what is wrong with Charlie's flat is duly forthcoming, as all them sex noises start up again, though Charlie is still his old oblivious self.

"Well, it might be more err…" starts Spandau.

"Saucy!" squawks Hadley.

I mean, where did he get all that from? How does that parrot know?

"Private, like," says Spandau, trying to cut the bird short.

"Yeah, more private… For everyone!" agrees Chen.

"More private than here?!" says Charlie incredulously. "What, with all them punters getting smashed off their faces in the pub down below? What is you talking about? Anyway, Spandau, what was it you was saying?"

"I was saying like *The Duke* might be…"

Charlie interrupts him. "No, no! Before that."

"About zombies?" asks Len with a note of surprise in his voice.

Chen pipes up. "Yeah, we were talking about how zombies is like Blue Sky Thinking, Charlie. However, I was saying that what happens in the cinema today, is like the Internet of tomorrow."

Charlie shakes his head. "What are you on, Chen? No. No. Before all that!"

Them sex noises is getting, well, very noisy.

Lenny, who is - let's say - closest to Charlie spits it out. Well, rather, he has a nervous cough and asks. "Doesn't this err… bother you, Charlie?"

"What?" says Charlie, "Spandau not remembering? Well actually…"

It's Lenny's turn to interrupt. "No, this." He tips his head over in the general direction of the bedroom door, several times, before Charlie eventually gets what he is talking about. Well, them sex noises is getting louder and louder.

Charlie gets the gist, finally. "Is that what this is all about!? Kyrstee having a good time with Reg?"

"Yeah, but…" says Chen, "you're, you know, you and Kyrstee, you're together. An item… Aren't you?"

"Yeah? And?"

"Well…"

"Well, what?"

Chen makes the argument as clear as he can. "Well!!"

Charlie takes a deep breath. "But I can't do it, can I? I mean, I can hardly stick it up her with a plastic tube poking out of my knob?"

"I suppose…" says Len, shrugging.

"And Kyrstee's a young girl, Len, she needs… satisfying. Reg is a decent enough bloke; clean, does a good job in the garage, trustworthy, doesn't pilfer. Well not much, only as much as… Well, as much as you'd want him to, else you'd know he was up to something worse. So, you know… No, I don't have a problem with it. Let them have a good time, I say. If anything, makes me feel better."

"Vicarious," says Spandau, chucking in a big word for intellectual effect.

"Saucy!" says Hadley again, more to the point.

"Well… I suppose," shrugs Len again.

"Yeah," agrees Chen, joining him in a shrug.

"I still think we'd be better at the err... *Duke*, Charlie," says Spandau.

"Leave the bloody *Duke*! We'll be needing that later, when we wants a bigger room for everyone. Now, what was it you was saying, Spandau? Back, before all that... zombie madness and... that Reg and Kyrstee's whatever?"

Spandau is flummoxed. Well, anyone would be with all that business going on next door.

"You was saying," explains Charlie, slowly and deliberately, and with his voice raised above the sex racket. "You was saying, that the only ways we'd get away with it, was if I was already dead."

"That's right, like zombies!" shouts out Chen.

What is it with him today?

"Will you put a lid on them bloody zombies, Chen!! No..." And Charlie takes out a crumpled piece of paper from his trouser pocket, you know the one what Doc Walker gave him just the other week. He holds it up. "Being dead," he smiles. "Now that might just be work..."

It's all about timing sex, innit? Well, just at that very triumphant lightbulb moment of Charlie's, the ecstasy point is reached next door.

Is that a good sign?

I don't know, but I do know it's high time they was all due a bit of luck.

...

## Chapter 8

Now, we come to a funny old time in the story, and it would take a lot of explaining. So much so, that you might end up putting this book down and popping down the local. And then where would we be, eh? I'd be talking to myself.

So, I'll keep it tight.

Now, picture this, or even better, if you've got it to hand, play it. I mean the music *Time is Tight* by Booker T and the MGs. 'Cause you see, that's what they is playing, that four-piece outfit in the purple velvet what was playing at Peter Fitzpatrick's funeral. Only now, they's playing down at *The Duke*, in the bar area on the ground floor.

Meanwhile - and there's a lot of 'meanwhiles' in this bit - young Reg is fitting out three new large mobility scooters in the garage alongside of an old coach. And Charlie is walking up and down with his stick. Definitely looking a bit more spritely now is Charlie, pointing, nodding his head, shaking his head, you know, offering advice.

At the same time, well different really, but at the same time within the context of the *Time is Tight*, Doc Walker and Charlie is in the mortuary of funeral directors *Deepe and Stiff* talking to the mortuary attendant, Clive, what is all dressed in his white scrubs. Never smiles, that morose mortuary geezer. I mean, I've heard tell them undertakers has got the blackest sense of humour in the book, but that Clive, well… a mystery. Or maybe just the exception what proves the rule. Anyways, Clive is opening and closing some mortuary drawers by way of demonstration. Doc Walker is doing a little explaining himself and, you know, offering his advice. Then there is the shaking of hands and a nice little plump brown envelope is passed from Charlie to that mortuary geezer, Clive.

Meanwhile, Chen is talking to a very ethnically similar young woman. Well, it's his daughter. They's in the back of a car in a dark corner of Brighton and Hove City Council car park. Spandau Barry is sitting quietly at the wheel. Chen's daughter hands over several rolls of what looks like wallpaper and then has a furtive look around. And would you Adam and Eve it? Another brown envelope changes hands.

Meanwhile - that's right, another one, though, well obviously at a different time - Charlie is driving around the Brighton *Lanes* on his scooter. Not one of them big reinforced jobs what Reg is working on, but on the one what he sorted after that graveyard... incident. And Lenny and Chen is with him on theirs. They's checking various buildings closely, stopping, talking in low voices at corners, entry and exit points, driving past Fitzpatrick jewellers, but taking care not to stop or look directly at windows. Instead, every so often Charlie checks his watch.

Meanwhile - and by now you knows what I'm saying - Spandau Barry is in a party shop somewhere, with Hadley as ever on his shoulder. He - Spandau that is - is picking through some very brightly coloured costumes like what a drag artist might wear. The shop attendant - what looks a bit like a drag artist himself - is all fussing about over Hadley 'til he gets a peck on the finger. That'll sort him. Well, Hadley is very discerning about who he's friendly with.

Then, we is back again in the garage with Charlie once more supervising Reg, who is now spray painting them new big scooters. And look, there's three large pots of red, white and blue paint on floor.

And then; well, well, well. We's got Pinkie, Bas, Coffee-mate, Mickey, Big Albie and of course Trevor - cap on his head - all arriving in Brighton, and coming out the station looking for their lift. Their own young boys'll be down soon enough. Bit of young blood required, but it's good to see the old team assembled for a proper purpose, and not just 'cause one of their company has gone to meet his maker. Spandau's come down to meet them in his 7-seater Estate car, the old Renault Savanna. They shake hands though the front window and then Pinkie and Trevor rush and wrestle to get in the front passenger seat. Well, it's a case of migraines versus asthma. However, whilst they is fighting each other like the five-year olds they is, Big Albie jumps in the front and they end up having squeeze into two tiny fold-up kiddie seats in the very back row. Well, if you behave like kids…

And meanwhile - the final one - we's got Charlie again, this time wearing a suitably smart light grey suit, complete with elegant wooden walking stick laid across his lap. It's got an ivory handle carved in the shape of an elephant's head, that stick. Wonder where he got that from. We'll never know. Well, unless someone asks him. He's sitting on a stair lift is Charlie, slowly ascending to the first floor of *The Duke*. Well, as you know, there's a big meeting room up there and *The Duke's* owners is always discreet, as long as it's not a Fitzpatrick involved.

Downstairs, that band has just finished what has been a rather tidy rendition of *Time is Tight*.

Nice one, lads. Nice one.

…

## Chapter 9

It's a neat little tune that; *Time is Tight*. Got a proper sense of purpose, resolve, determination, you know, without, well, without any feeling of panic. Just the job really and it sets the tone just perfect.

For it is a single-minded Charlie what has enjoyed a smooth and comfortable trip up to the first floor of *The Duke*. Well, that's a new stair lift. And look, it's just like them old days again with a very familiar cache of crooks sat 'round the table. As well as, you know, some of the next generation keen to broaden their experience and get in on the act. Though what exactly the act is, they is not yet fully appraised.

The blinds is all drawn, some maps and other information is stuck to the walls - Charlie's done his prep - the lighting is subdued, and what with the occasional puff of smoke, for tobacco is permitted in this scenario. This is a private room in a pub for crying out loud! The whole affair has a proper air of criminal intent.

"Time is tight, lads. Time is tight, for me, for you, for the whole operation," says Charlie, as he walks into the meeting room.

Naturally, there is mumbles of agreement and nodding of heads, as well as the various *'So how is you doing, old son?'* conservations coming to a close.

"A few things to get straight first, lads," says Charlie, standing at the top of the table and addressing the assembled. "Number 1: In front of you is your new phones; burners. Mickey, collect the old ones. I want them all! You only use these ones - the ones in front of you - until the job is over!"

Mickey duly obliges and goes around with a black bin bag collecting all the mobiles.

"'Ere, I got some nice photos on here, Charlie," says Trevor, scrolling down his screen. "Grandkids and that... Wouldn't want to lose them. You know I changed my phone once and..."

"You'll get it back, Trev, once the corn on the cob is all over and done," says Charlie interrupting him. "Now just put it in the bag."

Well, he don't half go on sometimes, does Trevor.

"Number 2: I don't want no-one going 'round them *Lanes*. Lenny, Chen and me; we's been all 'round them, shot the video, marked the route. There's CCTV cameras down there all over the place, and they hold digital data for two weeks. I don't want any of your ugly mugs poppin' up when the police start sniffing around. Understood? No checking out nothing. No souvenir shopping!"

There is more mumbles of agreement and nodding of heads.

"Three:" continues Charlie, - you can tell he's rehearsed all this - "Spandau here, has sourced our disguises from out of town. Thank you for making the trip, Spandau."

Well, Mr Spandau Barry accepts the compliment with a modest wave.

"So, I don't want no-one wearing their own gear," says Charlie emphatically. "Is that understood?"

Them mumbles of agreement and noddings of heads continues.

"What about my cap, Charlie?" says Trevor. "I always wear a cap."

"We'll find you another cap, Trevor, and a very nice one too. Now lads," Charlie stands up, holding onto his posh walking stick, "some of you know bits and bobs about this... operation, and some of you, well, you don't know much at all."

The latter state of affairs is confirmed by the usual vacant stare on Trevor's face.

"So, let me ask you," says Charlie, "what is the biggest day in the social calendar in this fair city of Brighton?"

Them mumbles is accompanied by shrugs and raised eyebrows.

"Christmas, Charlie!" pipes up Chen, like he's back at school and just learned to read 'Cat on the mat'.

"No, the Brighton Festival, Chen," says Lenny. "There's a lot of people come down for the arts festival, Charlie. Comedy, music, some very good acts too. I mean…"

"No, no Len," interrupts Chen. "It's gotta be Christmas… and New Year. I mean the town is jumping… Although, I suppose," and he has a brief moment of reflection, "when you think of it… at the height of summer, on a nice day, I mean you get trainloads of visitors and all sorts of…"

Charlie's had enough. Well, these two - Lenny and Chen - they is supposed to be the two accomplices what is most in-the-know. Mind you, he don't tell them everything, Charlie. Well, you wouldn't, would you? Still, what is they talking about?

"It's Pride!" shouts Charlie. "Pride! Bloody Pride, innit!?"

"Oh, yeah," says Chen. "Of course, Pride, very popular. Coming up soon if I'm not mistaken. Not my scene really, I mean Spandau, you probably…"

"Oh no, it's full of kids now, Chen," says Spandau, warming to a little theme of his own. "And like most of them are not even gay. No, they're just here to party and get hammered off their heads on booze and NOZ."

"Yeah," says Chen, and with some sympathy. "The place is a total mess the next day, I mean, I remember my daughter, she said you'd think…"

"Stop! Stop!" shouts Charlie. He takes a deep breath. "Focus lads. Focus."

They all sit up, you know, re-adjust, like they is now paying proper attention.

"Bloody Pride," says Charlie. "The city is buzzing. The streets is packed, there's a parade, big parade. You can't move. You can't drive. Couldn't get a blue light ambulance through it all last year, could they, when that young geezer died from a concoction of happy drugs?"

"It's true, it's true," they all agree, even them what don't live in town and has never been to Pride.

"So, is we all going to Pride, then Charlie?" asks Trevor.

Charlie shakes his head and takes another deep breath. He's going to need a few of them to get through this.

"Now," he says. "Each year, coincidently, at this very time - the time of Pride - the Fitzpatricks has a stock take. All the proceeds from the whole of the South Coast operation is transferred to them Fitzpatrick jewellers' shops in *The Lanes*. A balance of payments is taken, and a share of profits distributed to partners."

"What d'you mean, Charlie?" says Pinkie.

"The movements, cash flows, the differentials, the ins and outs etc. All the money that is laundered, - <u>laundered</u>, you'll know about that, Chen - laundered through them three poxy little jewellers' shops in *The Lanes*. That money is counted and all the dividends and shares and bonuses paid out to the various partners accordingly. It is the one time of the year when there is mountains of cash, in one place, at one time… Well, three places actually 'cause, as you know, them Fitzpatricks has got three shops."

There's a lot of quiet thoughtful nods. Well, nothing catches a crook's attention more than the thought of a lot of cash.

"Our job," says Charlie, "our job is to take it. And make off with it."

"Easier said than done, Charlie," says Bas. "I mean I don't live here, but I know them *Lanes*. Very pleasant. I've often wandered through them thinking you could cook up a nice little corn on the cob here. But them *Lanes* is narrow - too narrow for a car - and there's lots of police around, on racing bikes even."

"Very true Bas, very true, and that will present a particular challenge." Charlie stands away from the table and with his walking stick moves around the room, stopping to point it at the information displayed on the walls. "Now, you has all seen the film, *The Italian Job*. I mean the first one. The proper one."

They all nod. Well, everyone's seen it. I mean, who hasn't?

"Well," goes on Charlie, "these maps show our route into and through *The Lanes*, and - more importantly - our way out through the Brighton sewers. Thank you Chen, for obtaining this important information."

Chen smiles, "Well, I'm just happy to keep it in the family, Charlie."

After a nod of appreciation, Charlie continues. "Yes, *The Lanes* despite being tight, has got some of the oldest, and largest sewers in the city. Them Victorians was proud, didn't cut no corners when they built them. However, unfortunately, them sewers is still too small to hold a car, even a mini, a proper one, one of the originals."

"Shame," says Trevor. "'Cause like that film, well, it's like a true story, ain't it? I mean, it's based on proper fact like."

Charlie takes off his glasses and cleans them. Well, it's not easy with this lot, is it?

"However," he continues, "them sewers will take a smaller vehicle."

"Like what?" says Bas.

"Like a mobility scooter, Bas, a mobility scooter."

A few eyebrows is raised. Understandably.

"A mobility scooter," continues Charlie, "fitted out with the correct suspension, thrust, torque, centre of gravity etc. and so forth. Exactly what I've had Reg working on these past weeks."

"Why isn't Reg here then, Charlie?" asks Len.

"Reg…" sighs Charlie, and he's a bit more hesitant here is old Charlie. For like, well, this part obviously cuts him up a bit. "Reg cannot know about… the <u>whole</u> operation. For Reg, for Kyrstee… I don't want her to know nothing. She worries."

Charlie sits back down and sort of shifts uncomfortably. He's in a bit of pain, inside and out. "And quite rightly," he continues. "Well, she's a woman, ain't she? And therefore, and Reg, as her err… Well, you know…"

"Saucy!" says Hadley the parrot. Well, he does know.

"Don't seem fair, Charlie," says Len.

"Look," says Charlie, "Kyrstee is like, a beautiful, innocent butterfly. If she's involved in this, whether on her own or through Reg, then, you know, she's contaminated, she's soiled. And as you all know, it's a slippery slope, this crime business. No, Kyrstee and, by association, Reg, will get a tidy little honest sum - well, honest enough - from me, once I'm departed. And that will see them set up with a neat little garage and hairdressing business for the rest of their lives."

"It's an unusual combination, Charlie," observers Trevor, "cutting hair in a garage. Are you sure that'll work?"

Another Charlie sigh, but one what brings him out of his temporary melancholy. "Separate Trevor, separate businesses; one with the hairdressers, and the other one with the garage. So, all Reg needs to know is that we is cooking up a nice little corn on the cob, and that we need them vehicles to look and run in a certain way."

Charlie goes over and looks at the maps on the wall.

Pinkie stands up and joins him, "In a certain way," he continues for Charlie with a smile, "through them sewers while the city is grid-locked by the Pride parade?"

"Exactly."

Bas has a cough, you know, one of them 'excuse me' coughs. "Err... Charlie. Are you familiar with Deja-vu?"

"Does ring a vague bell, as they say, Bas."

"Well... Some of us..." says Bas. "Well, we know how that story ends."

"No, no..." says Trevor with that stupid smile on his face. "'Cause, I mean, like I heard they actually got away with it in the end."

"No, no!" says Mickey. "What happened was that they had to open the back of the bus and let all that gold fall out."

"Well, how is they gonna get to the back of the bus, then?!" shouts Coffee-mate. "I mean, the weight from just one person crawling…"

"Well of course they can!" interrupts Pinkie. "I mean…"

"Lads! Lads! Lads!" shouts Charlie. "Focus. Focus."

Well, focus is required, though you can appreciate that a lot of folks has got very different views about exactly what happened after the screen credits of that film *The Italian Job* was all done and dusted.

"The difference," says Charlie with some emphasis, "the difference with us, Bas," he says looking him straight in the eye, "is that we ain't got no Alps to cross. All we has to do is emerge from them sewers, make our way along to Beachy Head and Bob's your pride and err… well, joy."

There is more nods but it is fair to say that some of them nods is laced with a bit of scepticism.

Charlie carries on. "And most importantly, the money - the proceeds of our criminal endeavours - must then lie undisturbed for one year. That is the deal! Them Fitzpatricks and the police will leave no stone unturned looking for that cash. But as it is crooked cash, they will not be assisting one another. If anything, they will be getting in each other's way; makes our task all the easier. So, all we - you - gotta do is just wait! Wait! You must be patient and wait!"

"We got it, Charlie," says Bas.

"Now Spandau," says Charlie getting down to a bit of detail, "you will be overall logistics and control. I hope you don't mind missing out on the big Pride day."

"No, as I say, Charlie, for many years I haven't…"

Charlie interrupts, but politely you know, "You Spandau Barry, will be in the crow's nest, stationed on top of Sussex Heights."

"What, the Tower Block?"

"Highest point in the city, Spandau," says Charlie, "what will afford you the perfect view of all what is happening below."

"But what about Hadley?"

"Your parrot?"

"Yeah."

"Well, he can come along. Might appreciate a bird's eye view. You always take that bloody parrot with you everywhere, anyhows. What, you afraid he might fly off back to the jungle?"

"He can't fly far," says Spandau. "I keep his wings clipped."

"Well then?"

"Hadley's afraid of heights."

What?!" says Charlie, "a grounded parrot with bloody vertigo?!"

"Yeah."

"Well, you'll just have to leave him at home then, won't you?"

"But I never leave him at home…"

Charlie takes off his glasses and rubs his face. Where did he get this lot from?

"You could you try soothing him with music," says Lenny. "I know he likes music."

"What sort of music does Hadley like then, Barry?" asks Chen, genuinely curious.

"Well," says Spandau, "he likes the Pet Shop boys."

"That figures…" says Charlie determined to draw a line under this little interruption. "Well, Spandau, you just soothe his little nerves with some eighties synth-pop or bloody well leave him at home!"

Hadley says nothing, but he's a clever parrot and probably followed the whole conversation. Spandau offers him a couple of sunflower seeds by way of consolation, you know, in case he's been upset by the frank discussion.

Charlie resumes his walking and talking routine. "At various points…" - he taps the maps with his stick - "on the route, some of you - see your names here - will be required to close off an entrance or exit, obstruct, clear, etc. And I don't want no-one getting lost down them sewers, they is a maze. So, study these maps. It is all worked out and written down in black and white. You got five days to memorize it all, 'cause, though we got a lock on this room, these maps and papers is all for burning."

Charlie sits down again at the head of the table. "Time will be of the essence, lads. The alarms will sound and we will have just three minutes - three minutes - to gather together the proceeds of our… noble endeavours, then a further five to draw all the available police and their vehicles into *The Lanes* area. So that they is then stuck there, courtesy of the wonderful Pride parade. Whilst we disappear down them sewers, only to re-emerge, at some distance from the noisy, happy, gay, partying throng."

Trevor is excited. "Charlie, I like it. I like it! I don't see what could possibly…"

Charlie immediately shuts him down, well scared. "Trevor! Trev! Don't say that."

"What? I was just…"

Charlie holds out a threatening forefinger. I mean, who would have thought Charlie was so superstitious? "Don't," he says. "Don't. Just don't."

There's one of them pauses. Well, been a bit of a theme in this story, that.

"Who's fronting the robberies then, Charlie?" asks Big Albie.

"We will be paired, Albie. I will be with Trevor, Lenny with Pinkie and Chen with Bas. Lenny, Chen and me might be infirm, but we do know best how to drive them mobility scooters."

Chen rubs his hands with glee, "Oh, can I have my scooter fitted out special like a chariot, Charlie, you know like the one in Ben Hur?"

Charlie tips his glasses down his nose and fixes old Chen with a cold stare. You know, a sort of silent intellectual put down. Enough said. He carries on.

"Mickey, you will oversee the escape route, and you and those helping you, all of you still nimble, will follow us down the sewers on them two-wheeler electric scooters, the same as what litters this town day and night."

"So, we is going all electric, then?" asks Pinkie.

"All electric."

"I suppose," says Trevor drifting into serious thought. Well, serious for him. "I suppose, Charlie, we're like re-setting the criminal bar. I mean, like pioneering a new blueprint for future crime. You know. What is it? Low carbon emission crimes and all

82

that. Might be important in the future what with all them sea levels rising."

"That is true, Trev. That is true," says Charlie. "Not that them courts will take any notice of it if we do get caught, which we won't."

Well, that's what criminals always think.

"Now, Coffee-mate has sourced the necessary tools for the job. Thank you, Coffee-mate," says Charlie pointing the finger of appreciation at his old friend. "Now, remember, them firearms is for effect only! Not for serious use. Half of them don't even work proper."

"Well, it's very difficult nowadays," says a slightly offended Coffee-mate. "Ever since the IRA went all peaceful and that… And you did say we had to keep the costs down and…"

"Didn't mean to offend, Coffee-mate. Didn't mean to offend. You done a great job," says Charlie. "I'm just making the point that we don't need no-one being silly with them weapons. I don't want no-one getting hurt, least of alls, one of you lot."

Well, it's nice to know he cares, innit?

"And anyhows," continues Charlie, "makes no difference, guns or clubs, we'll all be done for aggravated burglary if we do get caught… But we won't."

Well, as I says, that's what all criminals think; else there wouldn't be no crime, would there?

"You, Albie," says Charlie, "will be responsible for the reception and transport of the said vehicles following our escape and arrival at the point of rendezvous." Charlie points over to one of the maps with his stick.

"Will do, Charlie," says Big Albie.

"Time, as I say lads, is tight, as are finances. There is no Mr Bridger. We do not have the luxury of practice, of smashing up vehicles, blowing up vans, etc."

"Shame," says Trevor.

"However," and Charlie is all smiling now, "if all goes to plan, and I am confident it will. We will emerge with over six million happy ones for us to share and enjoy through retirement. Or," and he cops a look at the younger generation, what - credit where credit is due - has been paying proper attention, "to give these young lads the start in crime what they deserve."

The young lads smile.

There's another one of them pauses as they all take it in.

"What if it rains?" asks Spandau.

"Rain?" says Charlie, puzzled. "Take a raincoat."

"No," says Spandau. "I mean, if there's heavy rain, the sewers all get flooded, don't they? I mean, that's why all that pollution ends up in the sea."

Charlie hadn't thought of that. He pauses. "Rain…" he says. "Rain? It's not gonna rain."

Yeah, like when did it ever rain in August in this country, Charlie?

The criminal entourage suddenly looks a bit worried. Charlie's their leader, and he quickly clocks their concern and realises he needs to address it pronto. Confidence is crucial in a job like this. You can't have no hesitation.

"Alright, alright, if it rains, we cancel. But it's not… It better bloody well not rain, that's all."

I mean it was a relevant observation from Spandau Barry, but you know, Charlie might have preferred to hear it in private rather than an open forum. I mean, it's a little bit undermining. But old Charlie is a pro and quickly picks himself up.

"Now remember, we only takes cash, no jewellery! These is all unmarked notes. The jewellery - apart from it being a lot of overpriced old tatt - will just give us away! So, leave it! This is a cash and carry job!"

"Shall we synchronise our watches. Charlie?" asks Chen.

"Nuts to your watches, Chen."

Lenny's still worried about, well… "Are you sure about Reg and, and err… Kyrstee, Charlie?" he says.

Charlie leans forward on the table, has another one of his sighs, heartfelt this time. "This is about us Len. It's a question of prestige, it's about righting some wrongs, settling old scores, making good the errors of the past. All Reg needs to know is that we got a nice little corn on the cob cooking - none of the details - and he'll be fine. Don't you worry about Reg, and don't worry about Kyrstee neither. They will inherit a nice little earner and enjoy a bright and happy future, free from the fickle hand of crime."

Well, he can be quite poetic at times, Charlie.

However, at this very point Charlie stops, though it is not for effect. No, he stops very suddenly, raises one hand to his chest, stands up, and tries to hold on to his posh stick firmly with the other hand, only to stagger.

Spandau Barry sees it first, "Charlie?"

Then old Charlie falls to the ground. And what a commotion follows. They all rush over to him like wasps round a jam jar. Hadley is spooked and flies up to sit on top on one of the blinds.

Lenny and Chen is a bit slow - naturally - to get over, but they get there and push in. Spandau bends down over Charlie.

"My tablets, my tablets…" croaks Charlie. He points at his jacket inside pocket.

Spandau Barry reaches in and pulls out some tablets. Charlie nods and Spandau tears one from the foil and slips it into Charlie's mouth.

It seems to have the desired effect, for in a few minutes Charlie is trying to sit up.

"I'm all right. I'm all right," he says. "Don't fuss, don't bloody fuss now."

"Are you sure, Charlie?" asks Lenny.

"I'm sure. I'm fine. I'm fine."

"Shall we call Doc Walker, Charlie?" asks Chen.

"No! I'm fine, Chen, I'm fine. Now Len…" Charlie reaches over to his old friend and takes his hand. "If anything <u>does</u> happen to me, and I tell you it just might, I want you… I want you to finish this job. 'Cause it's the perfect crime. It'll work. I know it will. Now promise me, Len. Promise me you'll do it."

Lenny is hesitant. Well, he's not a natural leader. I mean, none of them is, apart from the one what is currently half-poleaxed on the floor. "Charlie…" he says.

Charlie is hoarse with effort. "Promise me!"

"I promise, Charlie, I promise," says Len. But does he really mean it?

"Now let us call the doc, Charlie," says Chen.

"No, no. No doctor," says Charlie, struggling up onto his feet. "Leastways, not just yet. No, there's a couple of people I gotta see first."

…

# Chapter 10

So, just who is these people what Charlie Crystal's got to see? Well, happens that the first one might come as a bit of a surprise, even to old Charlie himself. 'Cause, well, if you had suggested this person to him just a few months ago, well, he would've laughed you out the room, or garage. But that's cancer for you.

So, there's old Father Scanlon sitting in his confessional at the Maculate Concept. He's come prepared 'cause these days, well, there ain't so many sinners wanting to shed themselves of their sins. They's more inclined to hang onto them. I mean, you forget about them anyway, don't you? Consequently, the old priest has brought along a few supplies for the duration: that is relevant newspapers what'll keep him company and some liquid refreshment. And as we speak, he's having one of his regular reads at the racing pages. He's got a blue biro. It's leaking. And in his considerations of form, what with putting that pen to his mouth and being lost in deep thought and what not, his lips is a bit blue now. Fingers is a bit blue and sticky too. As is the label on that half-empty bottle of whisky what always sits in the confessional corner.

Well, we all need a bit of sustenance, and not just the religious kind. Though that is exactly what brings his first and only customer of the evening into an empty church.

With no-one apparently about, old Father Scanlon has been thinking aloud. "Oh… *'Hound Dog'* in the 3.30 at Lingfield," he says with the beginnings of a smile, "now that might just have a chance… 32 to 1… Hmm… Never been placed… Well, I don't know, nine runners mind, might be worth an 'each way'…"

He rings that one with his leaky blue biro when the door of the confessional creaks opens and a certain Charlie Crystal clambers - well, more like hobbles - in and kneels down.

This comes as a bit of a surprise to Father Scanlon and with a cough he quickly folds his paper over the whisky, and sliding open his little wooden hatch, peers through the metal screen trying to see who it is what has just disturbed his racing studies.

"Err... Bless me Father, for I have err... sinned," says the sinner's voice.

Father Scanlon is quickly into role, well, you don't forget these things, half-way to dementia or not. "How long is it since your last confession, my son?"

"Oh... err... A long time, Father, a long time..."

And then the priest recognizes the confessor. Mind you, he presses his face right up against that metal grill just to be sure. "Oh! It's yourself!"

"You err... know who I am?" asks Charlie, a little bit worried.

" Of course I do!" The old priest rubs his hands with a mixture of satisfaction and excitement. "Well, well, well.... This should be good. I've had it just about up to here with little old ladies confessing their unkind thoughts. Sure, I haven't issued a penance worth more than two Hail Marys in the last six months."

"Oh..."

"And I hear you're dying, Charlie Crystal. Well... Nothing like the old death bed confession, eh? Oh yes, they all come crawling back in the end."

Charlie can hear the old priest's hands rubbing with glee.

"Ah lovely, just lovely!" the priest goes on, "Why, tis the perfect way to brighten up a lonely confessional. So... What exactly have you been up to all these years, Charlie Crystal? A lot of nasty business, I don't doubt."

"Well... I err..." says Charlie, "I take it that, if the err... If the State has seen fit to punish me, on the occasions of my err... the errors of my ways, then, they have - in loco parentis as it was - you know, been doing the work of The Almighty. And them sins don't really count no more."

"Well, I don't know about that..." says the priest. Naturally, he don't want to be put out of business by the long arm of the law. "I mean, it's not as if God has had any say in the matter."

"Well, then, I would hope, Father, that err... that err a custodial sentence in a hellish prison here on earth would remove any err... afford me err... immunity from further celestial prosecution, on the err... basis of double indemnity, etc."

"I'm not sure I follow you, Charles Crystal. I do know I haven't seen you at Sunday mass for God knows how long. Did you go to prison for that? And, I mean how do I - as God's representative here on earth - how do I know if you've made a genuine act of contrition for all them things that got you locked up for in the first place?"

"Well..."

"Contrition; financial or otherwise..." interrupts the old priest getting more to the point. I mean, he's not so demented, is he? "Just to be clear," he goes on, raising his voice so that if there's anyone else in church, they'll hear it alright too. But fat chance of that.

"Just to be clear, I mean," he says, "what about all that mess you made in chapel just the other day. I had to clean a lot of that up myself. Well, it was mostly Mrs Orr, the housekeeper, but... Well, I had to pick up the pieces of the Blessed Virgin, and neither she nor I were very happy about that!"

"Yes, I am, very sorry about that Father. I was sorely provoked, and I err... I assure you that I will make good with a substantial err... financial act of contrition very shortly."

"I'm pleased to hear it. Pleased to hear it. Now what about these other sins? There must be a whole host of them. I mean, how many years have you spent in prison?"

Charlie don't have to think. "Close on seventeen, Father. Well, you gets into bad habits…"

"Seventeen?! Seventeen?!" The priest can hardly believe his ears. "Now, well you must have committed some meaty sins. Probably, killed a few fellas, have you not?"

"Well, no, not that I know of…"

"I know for a fact you did a few jobs in Ireland."

"Yes, well, I did have to do a bit of travelling for work, Father."

"Ireland's a Catholic country, you know, Charlie Crystal! The Blessed Virgin herself popped down for a short holiday stay at Knock. Could you not have stuck to clobbering Protestants?"

"Well, I err… try not to discriminate, Father."

"Well, that's all fair and well, I'm sure."

But we all know it ain't.

Charlie takes one of his deep breaths. "Yeah… Well err… To err… get to my point, Father; what I wanted to know, is, well, whether it's possible err… to get err… forgiveness not just for past err… errors, but err… in advance of future ones?"

"Future sins? It's an interesting theological conundrum you pose there, Charles Crystal." He has a little self-satisfied think to himself, has that old priest. "You see, well, the Catholic Church has been at the forefront of plenary indulgences, since the Middle-ages really."

"What's that Father?"

"The Middle-ages? Didn't you go to school at all?!"

"No, the err… whatshisname, indulgences?"

"Oh, plenary indulgences," says the priest sitting back with a clever smile creeping across his face. "Well, there's various interpretations, but basically, we, the Church, sell you a little prayer card, and they have to be blessed by a priest, so they're quite expensive, mind. Anyway, they have a picture of a saint or the like on the front and a prayer on the back. You put it in your bible…" - Yeah, he thinks, what bible is Charlie Crystal gonna have? - "…or the criminal equivalent, and you say that prayer every day. You know, to build up your standing with The Almighty. So that when you do come to commit a sin, you've already accumulated some err… credit in your Offence Account as it were."

"I… I never knew that."

"Well, the fancy ones, the modernizers, you know," says the old priest with a look of mild disgust, "in the Church, they don't like us to put it about these days. They say it's old-fashioned. But old-fashioned…"

There's a reflective pause.

"Who's your favourite saint, like?" the priest suddenly blurts out.

"Well, I don't know that I've got one, really, Father. I'm a bit of a lost soul."

"Lost, eh? Lost? Well, St Anthony's your man. Patron saint of all things lost. Though I will say, I haven't found him so useful in recent times, especially since I've become a bit forgetful myself. I think old Anthony's become a bit fat and lazy up there. You know, been helping himself to a little too much of the milk and the honey, when he should be getting on with the business of answering prayers. D'you know; I accidently put my mobile phone in the fridge the other day - well, it's easily done - and St Anthony, well, he was no help at all. 'Twas Mrs Orr that found it in the end."

"Oh… I see… Well… What I err… What I also wanted to ask you about was, you know, if someone was to kill themselves…"

"Suicide?! Suicide?! Oh, now, that's a biggie, a big sin, a big one. Mortal. Though I've never heard it in the confessional, funny enough."

Charlie shakes his head, but, well, he knew it would be a bit like this. "I'm talking about if I was… If they was to err… help me out of my physical misery, distress, in a therapeutic way, as it was."

Father Scanlon's in like a shot. "Euthanasia? Accessory to the mortal sin?! Ah, well then, it wouldn't be you confessing, Charlie Crystal, it'd be someone else."

Charlie takes a deep breath, "Yeah, well, that's something I suppose."

Then there's another pause, well, they's both waiting for the other person to speak.

Charlie goes first. "You err… don't happen to have any of them Indulgence cards, do you, Father?"

Father Scanlon's not that much of a mug. "Well," he laughs with grunt, "only if you tell me a few fat sins first! Now, get on with it! And mind, don't spare me from any of the dirty details!"

Yeah, well, we'll have to give that bit a miss, I'm afraid; secrets of the confessional and all that…

…

Anyhows, now to the second person what Charlie needs to have something out with. And this one is less of a surprise.

For the very next day, Charlie finds himself in the passenger seat of a rather nice Jaguar XF saloon. You know, the Portfolio model with the higher-spec luxury trim. Bodywork come up good as new and you'd never know it was Category C. Well, the purchaser won't. Leastways, not with them new plates. It's parked up right up there on the South Downs looking down on a very lovely view, especially now the sun is just setting. There some woodland, you know, a nice little coppice, green fields and even a couple of windmills up there on the hill.

Charlie has his arm around his true love - well, his latest true love - Kyrstee, what has driven him here in the first place.

It's a very nice spot, and that's not lost on Kyrstee neither.

"It's lovely here, Charlie," she says, gazing at the colours of the sunset.

"Yeah, always loved it, Precious. My old dad used to bring us kids down here from London with my mum for picnics in the summer."

"Awe, that's nice."

"Not that often mind, only when he wasn't, you know, otherwise detained."

"Doing what, Charlie?" asks Kyrstee with, well, a little dream in her voice.

"Well, in them days, it was mostly mail-bags, but err, things have moved on."

"Yes, there's always progress."

"Yeah."

"I suppose texts and Tik-Tok and that have just about done it for mail-bags," muses Kyrstee.

"Yeah, that and the price of a first-class stamp."

The glow of the sunset lends a warmth to the two faces looking at it, Charlie in particular. Especially given that he hasn't looked quite so well of late, not since he collapsed down at *The Duke*.

Kyrstee turns to him and strokes his face. "Did <u>you</u> ever want to become a post-man, Charlie?"

"Err… What?"

"Like your dad?"

"Oh…"

Well, some things is not worth explaining. I mean, she's a lovely girl and all.

"Err… Funny enough, no," says Charlie.

"What did you want to be when you was little, Charlie?"

"Oh… I err… Well, I suppose… I was only ever going to go into the err… family business."

Kyrstee sits up and slaps him cheekily on the thigh. That hurt. Not that she seemed to notice. "So, you did want to work for the Royal Mail, Charlie Crystal!"

Charlie takes it on the chin, well the thigh. "Yeah, well, I suppose I did do a couple of jobs that err… involved, you know, the old GPO as it was back then. Not that they ever thanked me for it."

"Awe…" says Kyrstee, settling back. "I always think it's important to live your dreams, Charlie, don't you?"

Charlie wants to get to the point. "Yeah, well, what I, err… The reason I err… asked you to drive me here today, Precious, is err… to tell you that this is where I would like to err… spend eternity."

"What, in the Jag, Charlie?"

"No, no. Nice as it is and all… No, I meant, this spot. It's one of them woodland burials now, you know. You bury the coffin and then they plant a tree on top."

"Awe, that's lovely, Charlie, but a bit sad too… I don't like to think of you being eaten up by all them little worms."

"Yeah, well, doesn't fill me with the err… joys of life neither, Precious, but you know, needs must. And as you is Next of Kin, I mean, I just want you to be in the know, so as, you know, it all goes through smoothly."

Kyrstee snuggles up to Charlie. She's good at that. "Yeah…" she says.

"Good. And…" says Charlie, hesitating. Well, he has something else important to say. "Without wishing err… to put too much of a downer on the moment, Precious, I err… Well, I wants you to know… Well, Kyrstee…" Charlie stops suddenly and blurts out. "You are a lovely thing!"

"Thank you, Charlie!" she says, kissing him on the neck.

"'*Innocent as a rose*', as the song goes. And that is how I want to think of you, and keep you, you know, when I am, well, lying six feet under."

Kyrstee gives him a very sad look; bring a tear to a glass eye, that look.

"You know what I mean," says Charlie. "I won't be around for much longer, Precious, and my life has not been, well… It's hardly been an example, has it? And I don't want you contaminated!"

"Contaminated? Well, we never do it no more, Charlie. I mean the chances of me catching something from you now…"

"No, no, I mean… Kyrstee." It's another moment for a sigh. "Precious, I've been married three times, not been the best, err… husband, fortunately never had to be judged as a father. But… But… I am taking… I'm taking a stand with you, Kyrstee, if it's the last thing I do! And it might well be."

"What d'you mean, Charlie?"

Like Kyrstee is genuinely baffled and Charlie, well, he ain't exactly making it easy for her.

"I mean, I want you to know that I only ever wanted what is best for you, and you must always believe that!"

"What else would I believe, Charlie?"

"Good. That's settled then."

Well, I'm not sure it is. Anyhows, Charlie and Kyrstee is now locked in some sort of embrace 'til Charlie feels his old urine bag filling up.

"We should go," he says. "I got to pop down the Old Bill tomorrow about them charges."

"You were out of order in that church, Charlie."

"Yeah, I know, I know, Precious. But I err… I have squared things with Father Scanlon, and err… I'm trying to do the same with a err… Higher Authority."

"Well, that's something, Charlie… D'you want me to come along to the station with you tomorrow?"

"No, it's alright, I'll be fine. Them charges'll never come to nothing, and even if they do, I'll be long gone by the time anything sees the inside of a court of law. No, it'll be very straightforward, Precious. Can't see no problems there."

…

# Chapter 11

So, once more we's back inside John Street Police Station in Brighton, and a more harsher contrast with the beauty of the South Downs you'd be hard pressed to find.

And there's Charlie, sitting on a bench, on his lonesome in the waiting room. The sunset glow of the previous evening has left his face and he looks as pale as an hard-boiled egg.

He's come on his own courtesy of that new mobility scooter what Reg sorted, and he looks a bit nervous, does Charlie. Got a slight sweat on and he's fumbling about with the inside jacket pocket of what is an old suit. Maybe his nerves is jangling 'cause it's Sergeant Les Misérables what has been assigned to the desk today, I don't know.

Old Les is in the process of resentfully dealing with another one of what he calls 'your serial undesirables'. Not a categorization what is particularly clever or funny, but then again, you could say the same about old Sergeant Les Misérables himself.

Yeah, maybe Charlie's a bit spooked 'cause of old Les. Certainly, the sarky Sarg has a glance over at Charlie and lobs him one of his best looks of disgust. Honed to a fine art after many years of policing.

Charlie's having a right good old mumble to himself. "Why did I say that? Why did I bloody say that? *'Can't see no problems.'* What was I thinking? Bloody Trevor… Don't I learn nothing?"

He finds what he was looking for in his jacket pocket and pulls out a mobile phone. Time for a quick call.

"Hallo, Doc, Doc. It's me, yeah, Charlie," he whispers. "I think… yeah… this might..."

Then, he's listening intently. "Yeah... exactly," he says. "I mean..."

Then there's another interruption from Doc Walker and Charlie's listening again. "Yeah, yeah, of course. Down the Old Bill, John Street."

Then there's a bit more listening.

Well, them one-sided conversations is tricky. I mean, you can only hear half of any banter, can't you? Got to guess the rest. Anyhows, the exchange comes to a close soon enough.

"Yeah, yeah. Thanks doc..." says Charlie and he puts away the phone and slips one of them tablets under his tongue.

He really don't look well and if anything, that pill's made him look worse.

Old Les is finally done with his serial undesirable, but he continues at the desk, you know, farting around with his little laptop. Meanwhile, Charlie has now broken into a heavy sweat.

At last, the Sarg looks over. "Crystal!" he calls out.

Old Charlie struggles to his feet with his walking stick. He don't half look in pain as he shuffles across to the counter. Don't make no difference; Les Misérables is never exactly brimming with the milk of human kindness.

"What's wrong with you then, Crystal?" he asks.

"Don't feel so good, Sarg."

"You're not gonna start pissing all over the shop again, are you?"

"No, no. It's not that. It's here." Charlie points to his chest. "And here." Charlie points to his throat. "And here." Charlie points to his back. Now he's struggling to stand up. "Can I get a seat, Sarg?" he says.

"Oh, this is all I need," says Les.

Well, I think we all know what the good Sergeant needs...

The unsympathetic officer opens his counter to come out just as Charlie Crystal falls flat on his face, his teeth hitting the ground. A small pile of dust floats up. I expect that's where the expression come from.

"Crystal!" shouts the Sarg. "Crystal! D'you need an ambulance?" The copper kneels down beside Charlie, rolling him over onto his back and thinking to himself, 'There's no way I'm doing CPR on this old villain'.

"I called the doc a few minutes back," says a hoarse Charlie. And just at that moment - Thank God for that - Doc Walker rushes in complete with traditional brown leather medical bag in his hand.

"Doc, doc," says Charlie. "You gotta help, you gotta help me. The pain, it's too much, it's too much doc, I can't…"

I tell you; he's writhing about in agony, that poor man.

"What's wrong with him?" says the Sarg.

"A lot," replies old Doc Walker. "He's dying." The doc opens his bag up, fills a syringe from a vial and then injects it into Charlie's thigh, right through his trousers. "It's alright, Charles," he says. "It's alright."

Charlie's still groaning and writhing about, but then suddenly, in an instant like, he's all relaxed. It's like when you switch off a lightbulb. Well, not one of them new ones what takes an age to fade up or down, but one of them old traditional ones, you know, what behaves like it should. Charlie's face has become calm, you might say almost serene. And there's the trace of a smile across his lips.

"Oh," says Charlie, "that is helping. That is helping, doc. Thank you. Thank you…"

At this point his breathing becomes deeper, slower, like more deliberate. The old Sarg looks across at Doc Walker. He's a bit worried now. "What's happening, Doctor?" he says. "What's happening?"

"I told you," says the doc, "he's dying. That was just some pain relief."

Charlie's breathing is getting deeper and deeper now, sort of long, tired breaths. He reaches out and takes Doc Walker's hand.

"Thank you, doc. Thank you," he says.

"It's alright, Charles," comes back that reassuring Scottish brogue. "It's alright, now. Just breath quietly."

Which is exactly what he does. And a few moments later Charles Maurice Joseph Crystal breathes a peaceful last breath.

A silence descends on the scene. Only to be broken a few seconds later by old misery guts.

"What?!" he says.

"He's dead," says Doc Walker.

"What? Dead?" says the Sarg. "Is that it? Aren't you going to do any resus? I got a defibrillator just 'round the corner."

"Sergeant," explains the doctor carefully and with more than a modicum of authority, "the man's riddled with cancer, his bones are shot to bits with malignant tumour. You leap on him and start doing CPR now, and you'll just end up with a pile of broken bones on the floor."

The Sarg is, well, confused. "So, what are we gonna do?" he says.

"What do you suggest Sergeant? This is a police station, and I am a doctor."

"Well, what about an ambulance?"

"For a dead body? It's hardly an emergency."

"Well, we can't leave him here all day. I mean, I got things to do. I can't have a stiff littering the floor."

The good doctor takes a deep breath. "If you can get me one of your police vans, I can take him up to the mortuary. You don't happen to have the contact details for his Next of Kin, do you? I don't have his notes with me."

The Sergeant gets up to his feet, not that he's been a lot of use kneeling down beside Charlie. "Yeah, I do. It's some bird err… Nice girl, Kyrstee, err, with a Y, and a double E. Err… Smith that's it! I got her contact details back here."

Old Les nips back behind the safety of his counter.

"Well," says the doc, "if you give those details to me. I'll accompany Charles up to mortuary in one of your vans and give this Kyrstee Smith a call to come and identify the body. We won't be needing the coroner. I've been treating Charles regularly for some time now."

The Sarg is visibly relieved. "Yeah, yeah. You do that. You do that, doctor. I'll get you a van. Thank you."

Then he has a little aside to himself, has old Les Misérables. "Well, that's one less serial undesirable in Brighton…"

...

# Chapter 12

So, off we goes now to them undertakers *Deepe and Stiff*. That's right, we's in the mortuary, you know the sort of thing, you've been here before, albeit briefly. Yeah, all white tiles, stainless steel sinks and sinister drawers along one of the walls. Clinically clean but, well, you know, that weird smell.

And there's that mortuary attendant, Clive with Doc Walker standing by his side. They's chatting to Kyrstee, Reg, Lenny, Chen, Spandau and of course Hadley. Well, not directly to the parrot, naturally. It's the bird's first time in a mortuary and he's looking around, very curious. I'll be honest, I'm surprised they let a parrot in a place like this.

Reg has got his arm round Kyrstee. Chen's shivering. Well, bit of a chill in there, and in more ways than one.

Yeah, it's like one of them classic film scenes, you know, when the attendant opens a drawer and pulls out a tray with a body covered in a thin white cotton sheet. This tray's got Charlie Crystal on it.

Doc Walker lifts the sheet and there's Charlie pale face, eyes taped shut. I wouldn't say he looks peaceful, if anything a bit tense.

Kyrstee nods and then breaks down sobbing. Well, of course she would, she's a lovely girl and it's very sad. Reg gives her a hug. Let's hope it don't lead to nothing more. I mean, there's a time and a place…

"I am sorry," says Doc Walker. "Particularly, as you know, Charles was a good friend of mine. All I can offer in consolation is that the end was quick and peaceful. With his condition, it could have been… so much worse."

Poor Kyrstee is sobbing and snotting, I believe they calls it 'ugly crying' now, but I like to think of it as sincere. "You know," she says, "he was just talking about this yesterday, he was, Charlie. It was like he saw it coming."

"I'll write you the death certificate," says Doc Walker and he sits down at a desk and pulls out some sort of official book from a drawer. "That will allow you to get on and sort out his personal affairs."

Poor Kyrstee is suddenly shocked. "Charlie wasn't having no affairs?! Why he couldn't even…"

"Business affairs…" interrupts the doctor calmly, "bank details etc, you know."

Old Chen, he's shivering, and well, he's almost in tears too. He turns to Len. "You know what this means, Len? You know what this means."

Lenny is grim faced, and just nods.

"We gotta do it, Len," says Chen. "We gotta do it for old Charlie…"

"I don't know that I can, Chen," says Len.

Well, like I says before, he's not a natural leader.

Having finished writing out the death certificate, Doc Walker tears it from the book, folds it into a brown envelope with some sort of official address on the front - Registrar of Deaths or some sort - and hands it to Reg who's got one arm around a tearful Kyrstee.

"'Disseminated malignant cancer of the prostate gland'," says the doctor. "I promise you; it was as good an end as Charles could have wished for."

Kyrstee has another good old sob and then Reg leads her quietly out the door to that Range Rover what's supposed to be bound for Africa. The door closes, it starts up, and off they go.

"Terrible to think what a little prostrate gland can do, doc," says Chen.

The good doctor nods. "Yes."

"Is that 'cause it rotates, doc?" asks Chen.

"Sorry?" says the doctor.

"You know, rotates. I've heard that the prostrate gland rotates like a disco ball, you know, and that's how it fires out all them malignancies?"

They all look at Chen, seriously baffled. Well, it's not the first time.

Charlie - the dead Charlie that is - starts removing the tapes from his eyes. "You don't half talk a load of old cobblers, Chen."

Lenny, Chen, Spandau and even Hadley start back in a fright. Well, you would do, wouldn't you?

"Doc! Doc!" shouts Chen. "He's a zombie! Charlie's a zombie! It's… it's a zombie Acropolis!"

Charlie's almost sitting up now, helped by Doc Walker and Clive. "If you don't put a sock in that bloody zombie talk, Chen, I tell you, I shall personally see that it's you lying in here, and not me!"

"Charlie, you're not dead!" shouts Len.

"No, I'm not bloody dead! I still got a few more days left in me, and lot to get on with. Now, come on, I'm freezing in here, help me."

So, they all helps Charlie sit up proper and the sheet falls down over his knees to reveal an erect penis.

"Wow, look at that, Charlie," says Chen. "Frozen solid."

Charlie's surprised too. He looks down at his old friend standing to attention and flicks it with his finger. It makes a sort of icy-chinking noise.

"Well, would you believe it?" he says turning to the doc. "I mean, would it work, doc, you know? One last little day out together?"

The doc shakes his head sadly. "I'm afraid it would just melt away, Charles. And I'll need to put the catheter back in. I only took it out to stop you from freezing up from the inside."

"Shame," says Charlie. "Still, it's something I suppose."

And then he has a word, personal like, you know, with his old erect member. Well, together they's been in more than a few sticky situations over the years.

"Stand and salute old son," says Charlie, "for one last time."

And after an appropriate respectful pause Charlie turns to the doc.

"D'you know doc, for a moment down the Old Bill, I did wonder if I was gonna cop it for real, right there and then."

"Maybe one too many of those little pep pills I gave you Charles. I told you; go easy."

"Yeah, but they've given me such a lift, doc, such a lift."

They all look at Charlie and his erect todger, what already has got a bit of a Tower of Pisa lean on it. Still, it's been some time since they's all seen Charlie this happy and it brings a smile to their faces.

"Now, come on then, you lot," shouts Charlie, "get a bloody move on and help me up. I told you; I'm freezing in this death drawer! And we's got work to do!"

...

# Chapter 13

And they has.

    For it's now the day of the Pride parade, a day writ large in the heads and hearts of all those what live and work in the fair city of Brighton. Love it or loath it, you can't ignore it. Well, unless you bugger off elsewhere for the first week in August like a lot of punters do every year.

    And today, them *Lanes* is busier than ever, what with residents, visitors, day-trippers and what not. The flocks of the gullibles, as I've said before. And to be fair, they do add a nice little vibe to the place.

    There's more than one couple, holding hands, a bit of romance like, you know, joking, giggling in that lovey-dovey way. They's looking in them shiny windows at all that glittering jewellery, checking out the engagement rings. Smiling at the camera on the door before the shop assistant gives them 'the ok' and buzzes it open. Well, you can't be too careful, can you? I mean, them *Lanes* could be full of thieves.

    And look, there's a couple of policemen on their bikes. Short sleeve order today, and with special instructions not to come down too heavy with any roving reveller. Well, with the police force these days it's as much about reputation as it is about solving crime, innit? So, them coppers is cycling slowly, joking, chatting, giving it the old "Good Morning" and all that. "Can I tell anyone the time? Maybe give someone directions? Offer assistance across a road?" You know, the old community police officer routine.

    And would you Adam and Eve it? There's that saxophonist and drummer again, busking away to their little hearts' content. Well, with all them punters around, at least there's a chance of earning a few bob today. And the music? Well, you'll know it. It's an improvisation on '*The Self Preservation Society*'; a 1960s classic. Got a tidy little backing track as usual. Very nice. Very nice.

At some distance from this happy throng, Spandau Barry, has made his way to the top of Sussex Heights; that big ugly tower block what sits right on the seafront. Bit of an eyesore, but then Brighton's not short of them. He's got his binoculars in one hand and his burner phone in the other. Hadley, who's come along for the day actually don't look too spooked. Well, probably 'cause he's got these tiny earphones on, 'specially made. And you can just about hear, above the noise of the wind and the bands playing down below, the tinny sound of *Always on my Mind* by the Pet Shop Boys. He seems to like it, does Hadley.

Spandau Barry himself is closely watching the Pride parade as, right on time, it starts to move along the seafront. The parade will carry on towards the Pier and then take a sharp left onto The Old Steine, what sits just southeast of *The Lanes*.

Spandau looks slightly nervous but he can relax, for just at that exact moment, back in *The Lanes*, three large, beefed-up mobility scooters: one in red, the second in white and the third in blue comes bursting through three different sets of locked doors. Them doors may have got signs on them saying '*Entry by buzzer only*', but today that is an instruction what will not be heeded.

The scooters is all reinforced at the front with a sort of iron cowcatcher affair, you know, like on them old American Steam Trains crossing the prairie. At the front seat sits the driver - naturally - and at the rear, just like in them old Western stagecoaches, a passenger riding shotgun.

The three drivers and passengers is all dressed in colourful, flamboyant Pride clothing. You know, all puffed up, like some pantomime dame. And they's got facial latex and silicone masks on. Still, as this is Brighton, and it's Pride week, in the street they go unnoticed really.

Time it tight, and in a robbery - as any thief worth his salt will tell you - timing is all. So, as they bust through the front door of them three Fitzpatrick jewellers, the rear passengers draws out their shotguns, and fire into the ceiling. Bits of plaster falls down. Wonderful effect that.

Trevor lets out a "Yahoo!" Well, he would, wouldn't he?

The shooting is accompanied by loud instructions from the drivers. "Get down on the floor! Do not touch nothing! Get your bloody hands off them alarms!" And these instructions seems to have the desired effect, with the staff and customers all cooperating fully.

Having secured the scene, the rear passengers then dismount and make their way to the back room, where they each find a safe. Here, they do what any self-respecting robber would do and blow it open with plastic explosives. Those safe doors come flying off and don't half make a racket.

"Just stay on the floor! Face down! Face down and nobody gets hurt!" shout the villain drivers, and well, nobody wants to play the hero.

Trevor, what is sporting a particularly large and colourful cap, can't resist an observation.

"Only gone and blown the bloody door off!" he shouts back to Charlie.

"Get a move on and stop farting about," comes the sharp reply.

Charlie, like the rest of them drivers, disabled as they is, stays seated but bangs on the counter every now and then for effect. And it seems to be doing the trick. For all them staff and customers keep their faces down. If only they knew they was being robbed by some old age pensioners what would likely fall over in a light breeze.

The safes is emptied and banknotes stuffed into large holdalls. I tell you; there's quite a lot of money in there. Them

Fitzpatricks has been doing alright. And one by one, several holdalls is deposited into very large and specially mounted boxes on the rear of the mobility scooters.

Now, you will remember, Charlie was quite explicit. 'Only cash,' he said, 'no jewellery'. But there's always one, isn't there? Always one. And of course it would be Trevor. For just as he is coming out of the back room, he sees a nice little pair of gold and pearl ear-rings sitting on a counter. Well, I say nice, but they is well overpriced, and I don't believe for a second that the gold is 22 carats, but still, you know, they's quite attractive.

"Little memento," he laughs to himself, slipping them in the pocket of his outfit. "Little memento, that's all."

Once the box carriers is all secure, the drivers spin around and scoot out. Trevor and the other rear mounted passengers fire again into the ceiling. And now they's all laughing and whooping. Well, it's quite exciting robbing a jeweller's; gets the old adrenalin flowing. The whole thing takes less than three minutes. Timing.

The customers is still lying on the floor. However, as soon as them scooters depart, the staff, probably worried about their jobs as much as anything else, sound the alarm.

Charlie's red scooter passes the buskers on their way to the rendezvous point, and as if… well, as if by some sort of prior arrangement, that saxophonist dude and his drummer pal only just go and turn up the volume on *Self Preservation Society*. And they don't half 'give it laldy', as they say North of the Border.

I tell you; you couldn't make it up.

Well, with all them alarms going off, at this very moment, one of them two police officers on bikes suddenly puts his hand to his ear piece.

"We got an armed robbery at Fitzpatrick's jewellers on Hannington Lane!" he shouts.

Well, they both start cycling in that direction when the second one suddenly brakes and puts his hand to his ear. "Wait!" he shouts. "Another armed robbery at Fitzpatrick's jewellers in Meeting House Lane."

They looks at each other and is just about to split up when the first one puts his hand to his ear again. "What?! Armed robbery at Fitzpatrick's Jewellers in Clarence Yard! Somebody doesn't like those Fitzpatricks! And the robbers are travelling in mobility scooters?!"

"Mobility scooters?!" says the second copper. Then he speaks into his microphone. "Hello, control, we're gonna need full back-up here in *The Lanes*, bikes, cars, foot soldiers, the lot, all available vehicles. It looks like the whole *Lanes* are being robbed!"

After further explanation and a couple of them traditional fuzzy crackles – you know, what them police radios always do - a voice says, "Copy, all available units on their way."

...

Now, who doesn't love a good car chase? You know, the high-speed jinks, a bit of slow motion, camera shots from inside and outside the car, tense drivers, maybe some light malarkey, you know, a quip or two exchanged between the driver and navigator, and all those constantly changing external scenarios. And all of it - every single frame - shot lovingly with deft camera work.

Well, sadly this car chase is slightly different. For a start, there ain't no cars, just mobility scooters and push bikes. Nor is there any camera work, just me rabbiting on. Well, trying to extract as much action as can be got from some old geezers on disability vehicles scooting around some narrow lanes in Brighton.

But still, they is well souped-up them scooters, and the bikes is fast, and it's a chase. So, let's enjoy it.

In a matter of minutes there's a couple more police cyclists on the scene. They's come over from the North Laine, and they is all dashing about looking for them robbers.

The rendezvous point for Charlie and his team is the Quaker Meeting House. Well, seems proper, or maybe not, I don't know. Anyhows, them three scooters line up outside what is quite a nice building. Georgian, I reckon. You know, serene architecture. They all give the 'thumbs up', and off they go on their way.

As *The Lanes* is especially busy today, there's a lot of weaving in and out, with people jumping out the way and all that. I mean, them *Lanes* is home to several over-priced restaurants with tables and chairs laid outside. Hazardous for anyone with a visual impairment, I've heard say, and it is quite tight. Trevor, who hasn't had any breakfast leans out as they pass one table and grabs some food off a plate. What has he gone and got?

"A falafel?!" shouts Trevor with a heavy note of disappointment. "Bloody Brighton!"

And he chucks it away. Quite right too. I mean, it's not real food, is it, a falafel? More like a missile someone might lob at a vegan riot.

Now, in terms of stunts it has to be said that most of these is done by the police. Well, them scooters is very heavy. I mean, battery operated vehicles, they weigh a ton, don't they? And got very little lift. People say that they is part to blame for all them pot holes. And I mean, what with the age of the drivers; Charlie, Len and Chen. Well, come on...

But them coppers on bikes, well; very youthful, very nimble and very agile. And they has to be, 'cause you got Charlie's crew - as planned - creating obstacles all over the shop. You know; an emergency water mains work here, a couple of ladders there, manhole covers sitting askew right in the middle of the thoroughfare. And as a consequence, them police cyclists has to perform all sorts of wheelies, jumps, spins and skids just to negotiate all that. It's very exciting to watch. I'm only sorry you can't see it.

At one point, just as a copper pulls up alongside Chen and Bas in the blue scooter, Chen screams at Bas to press a button. Somewhat confused, Bas does as instructed. And would you Adam and Eve it? Out pops a spike from that mobility scooter. Well. I say spike, but it's more like a little metal stick really. Not quite Ben Hur quality. Still, it does the job, catching the spokes on the copper's bike and off he goes a tumbling.

"Thank you, Reg! Thank you!" shouts Chen. "I love it!"

"You ain't got atrial fibrination waiting 'round the corner," says Bas. "I'm not sure I can take much more of this!"

As they approach the Town Hall, the scooters go down some steps. It's a bit bumpy but as I say, them scooters is very stable. Also, happens there a nice little gay wedding going on at the same time. There's two grooms walking out the Registry Office each carrying a posy of wild flowers. I reckon they'll be very happy together.

In a matter of minutes, several police vehicles - cars and vans, and a few more bikes - pulls up at the various exit points of *The Lanes*. A senior copper - don't know her name, must be new - but she looks very efficient. You know, smart trouser suit, expensive haircut, Bluetooth earpiece. I'd say she was probably early 40s but looks younger, you know, works at it. Anyhows, out she steps from an unmarked car.

"Keep them back, keep them back," she says flashing her ID to the uniformed brigade. Well, naturally, a curious crowd has gathered and wants to know what's going on. Then that senior copper speaks into a microphone what's attached to her suit collar.

"All exits to *The Lanes* are now blocked," she says. "No possibility of vehicle ingress or egress."

Watching all this, with the aid of powerful binoculars from the safety of Sussex Heights, is Spandau Barry. He dials Mickey on his burner.

"That's it," he says. "We're on our merry way."

That's the code, see.

Then, in one of them back alleys of *The Lanes*, mainly occupied by bins, litter and the odd homeless geezer bedding down for an uncomfortable night, Mickey and Coffee-mate walk over to a big padlocked double metal doors affair with Brighton Corporation embossed on the front. There's plastic fencing across it. They pull aside the fencing, unlock the padlock with a key - well, Charlie did them the courtesy of fitting a new lock - and open the doors.

Moments later three mobility scooters appear from around the corner. One red, the second white and the third blue and without a by your leave, disappear through them open doors.

Mickey and Coffee-mate, cool as you like, then close and lock the doors and pull across the plastic fencing once more. They step back into a closed doorway and seconds later there's a couple of them police cyclists come racing around the corner. They speed right past them. After which, Mickey and Coffee-mate calmly pick up some little two-wheeled scooters of their own, open the door again, closing it quietly behind, and scoot off down the same sewer.

The various coppers on bikes is now all arriving at the different exit points of *The Lanes*, what is all now blocked by police cars. But where is them robbers? You got police officers looking all around, mystified. Them mobility scooters has just vanished into thin air.

And that efficient looking plain-clothes copper, well, she don't quite look so smart now.

"They can't have got out," she says. "We can't have missed them. They must still be in there. I want every property searched.

And I want all available routes out of the city; the A23, A27 and A259 blocked. No vehicle must leave without a search. The thieves must still be in there. They can't just disappear…"

But they did.

…

# Chapter 14

I'll keep this bit short. Well, it's not pleasant for the parties involved.

Now, if you's ever taken a trip along Dyke Road Avenue in Brighton, you will know that some of them houses is posh, very posh. You will also no doubt know, that just 'cause you lives in a posh house, it don't mean you is posh. More to the point, it don't mean that everything what you done to afford that posh house in the first place, was honest and above board. No, in fact, chances are, quite the opposite.

And so, here we is in the Fitzpatrick's Dyke Road Avenue residence. D'you know they've got a butler?! You know, posh old grey-haired geezer with an accent to match, tailcoat, drinks on trays and what not. I mean, who has a butler these days? 'Cause, well, should be obvious by now, they're not posh, them Fitzpatricks. Certainly not posh enough to have a bloody butler.

Anyhows, in that house at this very moment there is a lot of villainy all sitting round a big table in a big room with not much else in it. Well, it's a meeting room, see. 'Course, it's got a projector, computer, printer, efficient Wi-Fi and the like, but not a lot else by way of creature comfort. Hence that old butler comes in every now and then with some required refreshments.

The walls is painted an emerald green, like most of the Fitzpatrick house. Brenda is sitting at the top of the boardroom table, chairing what is the annual shareholder discussion on the progress of the various Fitzpatrick businesses across the patch. One of her franchised villains is giving his report.

"Well, the thing is boss," he says, with a note of, well, trepidation in his voice, "the thing is, Hastings… Hastings… It's a bit dodgy at the moment…"

Exactly what it is about Hastings what is 'dodgy' we's unlikely ever to find out. For at this very moment, Paddy - what Brenda has decided is no longer necessary at these important discussions on account of him being an idiot - rushes in, and without knocking.

He's breathless, and he's still got his arm in a sling. Brenda don't look too pleased about this little interruption. She's gonna be even less happy when she hears the news.

"The jewellers!" says Paddy, all puffing and panting. "The jewellers, all three of them! In *The Lanes*! Broken into. Armed robbery! Robbed! The money! Our money! It's all been taken!"

Brenda don't say nothing and then she stands up with what you might call a dawning realisation. "Crystal!" she says. "Crystal."

"The police are crawling all over the place," says a still puffing and panting Paddy. "*The Lanes* are all blocked off, but they can't find them."

"Police?!" says Brenda, spitting the word out. "Fat lot of good that'll do us. And anyway, if Crystal planned how to break in, he planned how to break out. He's not as stupid as he looks."

Well, it is what people say, innit? They say, 'Not as stupid as he looks.' But I mean, in this particular case, Charlie, you know, well, he don't really look that stupid. Actually, he looks quite intelligent if you ask me. I mean, if it was Trevor, or Chen, and they had cooked up a little corn on the cob like this, well, you'd be entitled. But, as I says, you could argue Charlie is actually <u>more</u> stupid than he looks. But - 'not as stupid as he looks' - it's what people say. And I'll leave it at that. Well, not really the best time to pick Brenda up on a point of order. If ever there was such a time…

…

# Chapter 15

Now, that copper in charge was right about one thing; you can't just disappear. But you can go underground.

Happily, it hasn't rained in days and the forecast is actually quite pleasant. Sunny intervals, some light cloud, but very little chance of precipitation. Makes for a happy Pride Day and a very happy Heist Day.

So, them mobility scooters is making their merry way along the Victorian sewers of Brighton what is all nice and dry. Well, almost. And since the Pride parade is blocking off traffic all the way from the Old Steine right up to Preston Park, well, getting across town, unless you is underground or can fly better than Hadley, is a problem.

'Cause well, you got police cars with sirens blaring and lights flashing trying to get through them crowds of Pride party-goers. But that colourful column of fabulous floats is as long as it is daft, filled with unrestrained revelry. There's a lot of alcohol knocking about, NOZ canisters and more than a few lines of coke. And hence there's also a lot of joking and grabbing at police hats and hugging them officers. Well, they will insist on this light-touch policing. 'Reputation' as I says, gets you nowhere. And them police officers above ground is getting nowhere fast.

Meanwhile, underground, them 'steady as a rock' mobility scooters is cruising along cavernous Victorian brick tunnels, lit today by their bright headlights. And the rest of Charlie's team is following in their little two-wheeled jobs, you know, bringing up the rear.

The shallow sewer water is all splishing and splashing, and watching it all there's the odd little vermin. Well, several actually, and they is quite sizeable as a matter of fact. They do say that in Brighton, rats is now more common than Estate Agents.

"Bet it's not as smelly as them Italian sewers, Charlie," shouts Trevor; making an irrelevant observation what is based on no knowledge whatsoever.

"Well," shouts Charlie in reply, "that's all your olive oil, Trev. That's what that is. Mind you, cop a load of that. Take out the bloody Titanic, that would."

And he's right, as he points out a large fat-berg with all sorts of disgustingness caught up in it. Yeah, give me olive oil any day.

Back up on Sussex Heights Spandau Barry is watching the scenes of confusion with some satisfaction. Looks a bit more relaxed now, does Spandau. And Hadley's as calm as ever. The parrot's moved onto Soft Cell with *'Tainted love'*, and seems to be enjoying it. What goes on in that bird's head, eh?

Spandau points them binoculars eastward and soon sees three scooters come bursting through a couple of white flaky painted wooden doors what opens onto the far east end of Brighton beach. Their exit is the signal for Spandau to make his own way down along the beach, courtesy of another two-wheeler scooter, to the next rendezvous point. That Hadley enjoys the scooter ride. Well, it's breezy, almost like flying. Brings back the memories.

And now all them scooters is out in the open, well past the parade, and turning on the style. Swinging to the left, swerving to the right, in and out of them Madeira Drive archways. Grandstanding, I say. And why not?

And look, you got families, children and old codgers all sitting on that toy train what runs on the Volks Electric Railway. Well, they's all thinking this is just part of the town celebrations, and they is waving and smiling and laughing at this mini mobility scooter Pride parade.

The scooters pass the nudist beach; at speed I say. Well, with all that old geezers' clobber on display there, you want to pass it pronto. I tell you, it's not what was intended when they opened that beach. Anyhows, before you know it, them robber vehicles all pull up into an old builder's yard where they find Big Albie sitting patiently behind the wheel of his converted bus.

Standing alongside is the rest of the team and their young lads. And it's not long 'til everyone, including Spandau Barry with Hadley on his shoulder is all back together again. There's a lot of congratulations, joking, back slapping and laughing. But as Charlie is about to remind them; they is professional thieves and the job is not done yet.

Big Albie opens the back of the bus and a ramp comes down. Charlie and the rest of the mobility scooter drivers pull up alongside it.

"Right!" shouts Charlie. "All you lot riding shotgun, off!"

"What?!" says Trevor. "Ain't we gonna drive up into a moving vehicle, Charlie?"

"Why for, Trev, may I enquire?"

"Well, excitement, of course."

Charlie tries to give Trevor one of his withering looks but he's a bit too happy for that to work proper.

So, then Charlie is the first to reverse up into the bus. His scooter plays that safety feature, you know, the beep and that automatic voice repeating, *'Caution, this vehicle is reversing. Caution, this vehicle is reversing.'*

"I thought I told Reg to get rid of that bloody racket," says Charlie. But still, it don't really spoil the moment. Lenny and Chen follows and the three of them gets off and steady themselves by grabbing onto their walking sticks, what has handily been placed up there for that very purpose.

"If it's any consolation Trevor," shouts Charlie down to his shotgun rider, "we are gonna chuck the scooters off a cliff."

"Ooh..." says Trevor, excitedly.

Will he ever grow up, that boy? I doubt it.

"Now, you lot," says Charlie to the rest of the team. "Up here and shift some cash!"

...

# Chapter 16

Well, with the help of them younger lads it's not long before all them holdalls has been unloaded and the cash placed very neatly in - would you Adam and Eve it? - a coffin. Nice piece of wood, that coffin. You know, dark mahogany, brass handles, decorative mouldings and panels, satin lining. Looks very comfortable, solid, and a fair old size too. Would be a couple of decades before any worm could find his way through that one.

And I should mention that in the course of transferring all that money into a coffin, Trevor also happens to tuck in that little pair of pearl earrings.

"I'll see you in a year," he says with a smile.

Just as well, I say. Just as well. We don't want no silly mistakes.

And now, well, it's more laughter, excitement and joking at the robbery success. Naturally, a few crates of beers has appeared, and everyone is quickly relaxed. Does that remind you of anything?

Only with this lot, they's not winding their way through the Alps. No, they's just on a short jaunt along to Beachy Head. As Trevor might say, 'What could possibly go wrong?'

Charlie is standing at the front of the bus, keeping his head. Though that don't stop him having a jokey little word with the driver.

"Now Albie, this ain't no Alps. So, no swerving!"

After all these years Big Albie's still got that majestic deep laugh. "No chance, Charlie! No chance!"

And before long, that old bus full of happy robbers drives onto Beachy Head. I say 'onto' 'cause when they arrives there, the bus leaves the road and travels over the grass. This is a tricky bit. The joking stops and they is all focused on the task in hand.

Big Albie parks up the bus, opens the back doors again, the ramp comes down and one by one, they push them mobility scooters out. Well, they don't half crash over the edge of that cliff onto the beach below where so many depressed individuals has sadly and conveniently jumped to their deaths before. After that, the lads chuck them two wheeled scooters out too. And down on the shore, the waves and rocks is smashing all them scooters - and any evidence - to bits.

It's all going so well, innit? Too well maybe… I mean, in a story like this, you just know something's gotta give. And of course, it does.

'Cause, it's like, you know how they say that a butterfly flaps its wings in the Amazon and there's an earthquake in Australia or whatever? Chaos theory, I believe they calls it. Well, I don't know what caused this unfortunate event, but suddenly that Beachy Head cliff edge starts to crack and crumble. To be fair, that sort of thing does happen all the time on the South Coast. It's the chalk, see, very porous. Probably nothing to do with any Amazonian butterfly. But whatever, that ground starts to shift, and the bit what falls off? Well, that is right under the bus.

Marvellous. With half the ground disappearing under it, that bus spins on a sixpence and before you can say 'seen it before' it slides down the grass and what d'you know? There it is, perched, balancing precariously, as they say, on a cliff edge.

"Oo-er," says Hadley.

"You have got to be joking!" shouts Charlie. "You have got to be bloody joking!"

But it is no joke. And not only is the bus stuck, but that coffin - that's right, the one with all that lovely money tucked inside - well, it slips to the rear of the bus. Whilst Charlie and his not so happy now robbers, well, they is all up at the driver's end, all strewn across the floor.

There's a lot of groaning and of course a few geezers has taken a bit of a knock or two. Well, as I've said many times, some of them is a fair age.

"No, no. This is not gonna happen..." says Charlie.

Time for one of them pauses, again.

After a few minutes with that bus swaying up and down, Charlie gives them drill. They're familiar with it of course. Well, they's all been to the cinema or seen it on the telly.

"Right lads," says Charlie. "I want you all to move towards me at this end of the bus. That way, we will counter-balance the money and stop it from taking us all over the edge. And keep that parrot under control Spandau, I don't want him knocking things about."

As if. Hadley's been the perfect flightless bird all day.

So, I mean, I need hardly describe it, the lads rise slowly - well, Lenny and Chen is bum-shuffling - and move very gingerly to the front of the bus. The bus sways, and, well, you know what's coming. That's right, that coffin slips even further away to the rear of the bus what is dangling over the cliff.

"Gently! Gently!" says Charlie, "further this way, lads."

And now them robbers is all congregated right at the front of the bus, but it's still swaying and you're right again; that coffin has slipped further away than ever.

Time for a bit of pessimism and a few recriminations.

"I knew it. I told you, Charlie," says Bas. "I told you."

"He did," says Trevor. "He did. Bas did warn us, Charlie."

Charlie's thinking, well, he must have thought about this a thousand times.

"No Bas. No. It's not gonna happen. Right… Right… OK. Listen lads. I got a great idea…"

Them robbers all groan. Well, they know that that means. Could leave them there forever.

"No lads, no. A <u>proper</u> idea."

That don't stop another big collective groan.

"No, listen. Listen!" says Charlie. "This time, this time, what we're gonna do is err… At my count of three, everyone - everyone what still can - is err… going to jump, jump up very high, and all at the same time."

They look a bit confused, them robbers. Well, a lot of them do at the best of time.

"But Charlie," says Lenny, "if we jump, it'll just make the bus lighter and we'll all go over the edge."

"No," says Charlie. "No."

'Cause, as I says, Charlie's thought this over countless times, especially on those bored, dark, lonely nights, lying in his bunk, banged up in Brixton.

"It will only be lighter momentarily, Len," says Charlie. "Then when we all comes down, our force will push the front wheels down as well and we can get a grip."

He turns to Big Albie. "As soon as we jump, Albie, you hit that throttle hard, maximum revs."

"Will do, Charlie," says Big Albie.

"We're gonna hit the bottom of the cliff, Charlie," says Bas.

"No, Bas. No."

A pensive pause arrives, you know a 'what will be' pause.

"Look," says Charlie, trying to shake them up. "Who's in charge here?"

"You are, Charlie," says Lenny, and you'd think he might have more of a note of gratitude in his voice. I mean, imagine it was Len, or anyone else for that matter.

"Well," says Charlie, "we all jump when I says 'jump'!"

"Jump to our death, maybe," says Pinkie.

"Jump when I says 'jump'!" repeats Charlie.

There's a return of that pensive pause. Well, hardly surprising. A few of them robbers is now contemplating their own mortality. Existential, as Spandau might say.

"Ready?!" says Charlie.

There's some mumbles of 'Ready'.

"Right," says Charlie. It's a tense moment. "On my count of three, everyone - everyone what can - jump. Ready?"

They nod.

"Right. One. Two. Three. JUMP!"

Them robbers jump, well, the fit ones do, and some of them younger lads really puts their backs into it. And as Charlie predicted, the bus tilts further over the cliff edge, but almost immediately as the jumping robbers land, bounces right back the other way. Big Albie slams his foot down and the wheels grip the ground beneath them. Front-wheel drive, see. And would you Adam and Eve it? They drive safely back onto the grass.

Well, what a cheer goes 'round that bus, what a cheer. All except for one person, Charlie Crystal.

"Why did <u>he</u> not bloody well not think of that!" he says.

But come on Charlie, now is not the time for getting upset over a stupid film.

…

# Chapter 17

Now, there is goodbyes and there is goodbyes. Some of them is sadder than others. And it's funny, all of them villains, you know, they knew this moment would come, but that don't make it no easier.

So, Big Albie's parked up the bus neatly in what looks like another rundown yard. There's a big steel drum sat right in the middle of the forecourt and Charlie and all his robber accomplices is tearing off their clothes like they is exotic mourners at some tropical funeral. They's pulling at their latex and silicone make-up and masks, and throwing the lot, along with their burner phones and them dodgy firearms into the flames. Not the bullets, mind. Well, might cause an accident.

There's three cars parked in that yard too. One of them is Doc Walker's Volvo; a nice Countryman Estate. Well, they last for every, don't they? A friend of mine clocked up over two hundred thousand miles on his. Still ran as sweet as the day he bought it. The second car is Spandau Barry's old Renault Savanna, well, not quite in the same league, but does the job. And there's an hearse from *Deepe and Stiff* with that mortuary attendant, Clive, at the wheel.

Doc Walker is sitting composed, stately, calm as ever. Just like his car, I suppose. You know, watching everything, quietly. He's got his brown leather bag in the back.

Clive, the mortuary assistant is, if anything, even more expressionless. Just sitting there, waiting.

Charlie, well, he looks more pained, though he's still in control and encouraging. "That's right, lads," he says. "All evidence into the flames. Everything, everything is for burning. No souvenirs! I mean it. No evidence!"

And them flames roar high. Nice colours too. Probably all that silicon-latex-plastic whatever, you know, hydrocarbons, pollution. Still, very attractive. Sort of northern lights in flame form.

Once they is all changed into their own clobber, the mood, what was one of triumph, is suddenly sombre.

"This is it, lads," says Charlie. "This is where I say goodbye… for real."

They all look at Charlie, sad like. Well, thieves and villains can be quite emotional, you know.

"I can honestly say," says Charlie, "and let's face it, in my life I haven't said that much honestly, but I can honestly say this; you have been the best. <u>You</u>, you lot, all of you; you have been the best."

Trevor is the first to be overcome. "We're gonna miss you, Charlie." He pulls out an inhaler and has a good old puff.

"Yeah'" says Bas, choking up. "I always knew we could do it, Charlie. I always knew. I said that."

"Yeah, Bas, well, sometimes," says Charlie, "sometimes it just takes a little longer than you first think."

Charlie turns to the whole group. "I'm gonna miss you all. But I know that, well… looking at some of you, you won't be too far behind."

They have a laugh and, well…

Now, your average South London villain is not much for embracing. But let's face it, the 'man hug' has crept into modern life, hasn't it? Personally, I prefer a strong handshake, but, well, sometimes, like in situations like this, I do see the point.

So, they all embrace old Charlie and fair dos. All that is except for Lenny, Chen and Spandau Barry, what is coming with him in the car on the final lap.

"Load it up," says Charlie.

And like natural pall bearers, that crew picks up the coffin from the bus and loads it into that back of that hearse. Lenny and Chen clamber into the back seats of Spandau's car, Charlie gets in the front, and Spandau Barry takes the wheel.

Charlie rolls down the window, a parting piece of advice; very important. "Now remember, and I mean it! One year. One year. You give it one year before you dig up that coffin. Else... else I will come back and haunt the whole bloody lot of you!"

They nod, they smile, and they sheds a tear. And the funeral procession - that is, the hearse, the Volvo Countryman Estate, and the old Renault Savanna - drives off.

...

## Chapter 18

The mood is somewhat different in Charlie's flat above the garage. Well, Brenda, Paddy and an entourage of obedient thugs has just arrived. They is not best pleased. Well, they's been robbed and trying to get across town over to the garage, what with all that Pride nonsense going on, well, it hasn't been easy.

They announce their arrival by kicking up a fuss. You know, throwing things about, pushing things over, generally making a bit of a racket. The usual.

Upstairs, Kyrstee and Reg is sitting at the coffee table, though it is tea what they's drinking. They look at each other with a 'What's that?' expression.

It's not long before they is fully informed of just who has arrived, when Brenda, Paddy and their accomplices march into the flat.

"Where is he then?" says Brenda. She's angry, and is wearing her very best threatening look. Though, to be fair, Reg and Kyrstee don't look too threatened.

"Who?" says Kyrstee.

"You know who I mean, Crystal."

"Charlie?" says Kyrstee. "He's at the undertakers."

"The undertakers?"

"In the mortuary. *Deepe and Stiff.*"

"What… Why?" Brenda's been thrown by this piece of news.

"What's he doing there?" asks Paddy.

"He's dead," says Kyrstee.

Brenda can't believe it. "Dead? What d'you mean he's dead?"

"He ain't alive no more…" shrugs Kyrstee.

Well, 'Well said, Kyrstee', I say. Couldn't be clearer.

Brenda is now completely baffled, and being baffled and angry don't sit well together. You know, don't make for logical thinking and decision-making.

"When did? How? Huh…"

Kyrstee does her a favour and explains quietly. "Charlie died yesterday morning, peacefully, at the police station."

"The police station?!" says Paddy. He can't believe it neither.

"Yeah. I got his death certificate here. I identified the body yesterday."

"Let me see that!" says Brenda, snatching the envelope out of Kyrstee's hands.

She rips it open. I mean, a little bit of respect please, even if it is for your enemies.

Brenda is understandably furious. That's her theory shot to bits. If Charlie didn't do the robbery, then who did? She scrunches up that death certificate and chucks it on the coffee table, fortunately missing the mugs of tea.

"I want to see that body," she says. "I want to see that body."

Well, some people is naturally very suspicious.

...

Of course, it is true, Charlie is at the mortuary, though not yet quite dead yet. No, he's lying on an open tray once more, though dressed now in that smart grey suit.

The mortuary attendant, Clive, along with Doc Walker, Lenny, Chen, and Spandau Barry with Hadley on his shoulder is all standing around him. And that mahogany coffin with all that lovely cash packed inside is sitting on supports alongside.

It's time for the final farewell.

"Goodbye lads" says Charlie. "It's been a lot of fun."

They is all lost for words, but the parrot speaks up.

"Saucy!" says Hadley.

"Yeah, it's been that at times too, Hadley," says Charlie, "though sadly not too much of late. Still, this suits me down to a tee."

He has a little shifty on the tin tray.

"This is actually quite comfortable, you know. I reckon I can rest easy here for a year, you know, before the switch." Charlie looks over at that mortuary attendant. "Now, don't you let them take me out before that!"

He has another little shift and a shiver. "Just a bit on the chilly side, that's all."

"Well, I told you Charlie, that's why I always wear a vest," says Chen. "Maybe you should put one on now."

"I don't think a vest will be necessary," says the doc.

"No, I don't think so, doc," agrees Charlie quietly.

They's all smiles, but them smiles sit a little uncomfortable.

"Right, Doc," says Charlie. "Do the business, if you will."

The old doc is quickly at the ready, and draws up a syringe from some vials in his brown leather bag.

"Saved me the price of a ticket to Switzerland, doc," says Charlie. "And you's no idea the trouble people like me has trying to get in there! Oh, wait."

Charlie reaches inside his suit jacket pocket.

"This err… This is for you, doc." And he hands Doc Walker a plenary indulgence card with a picture of St Anthony on the front and nice little prayer on the back. The doc takes a look at it, and is a bit puzzled.

"I'm Presbyterian you know, Charles?"

"I don't think St Anthony'll mind."

The doc slips the card into his trouser pocket, then puts the syringe into the back of Charlie's hand and injects.

A few seconds later, Charlie is drifting off.

"Nice…" he says. "Very nice…"

Not exactly the famous last words of a notorious small-time villain, but comforting in their own way.

And it's not long after that, that a couple of large cars filled with Brenda and company arrives at pace, skidding into the car park of *Deepe and Stiff*.

They's just missed Doc Walker, what's left in his Volvo, but their minds is focused elsewhere anyhows. They leaves the cars and burst into the undertakers making their way straight to the mortuary.

Lenny, Chen and Spandau Barry with Hadley is still all hanging about in there with that attendant, Clive. Well, takes them a little bit longer to get sorted and back out into the car and what not. They look a bit surprised - well, worried might be more accurate - at the arrival of Brenda.

"Where is he?!" she shouts. "I wanna see him! I wanna see Crystal dead."

There's a look of concern on the faces of Charlie's old friends.

"Where is he?!" insists Brenda.

Chen - a little bit timid it has to be said - points to one of them drawers. "He's in there," he says.

Brenda gives a very clear instruction to Clive, the mortuary attendant. "Open it!"

Clive opens the fridge door and slides out the tray with Charlie, covered in a white cotton sheet. He pulls back the sheet, as I says, like they always do in films, to reveal the face of a dead Charlie Crystal. Proper dead this time. Funny thing is though; he's just gone and died with a big grin fixed to his face.

Brenda can't believe it. "Crystal…" She's almost falling over, and I tell you it's not with grief.

The tray is slid back in, and Brenda paces up and down breathing heavily and cursing angrily. Then she stops right by that mahogany coffin.

"Is this for him?" she says.

The looks on the faces of Charlie's friends would not – as they say - win any poker games. They nod. Brenda taps on the coffin and flicks the tassels on brass handles, then she has a fiddle with the lid. Of course, they's all thinking; 'she's gonna open it'.

But she don't.

"Typical," she says. "Piece of crap. Never had any class, Crystal…"

Then she turns to her lackeys.

"Come on!" she shouts.

And they do. They all leave.

…

## Chapter 19

Now it can take quite some time to get 'round to a burial in today's merry England. Not on account of any merriment, you know, wakes or whatever, but more as a result of all that officialdom, lack of resources, under-funding and what not. The usual. So, there is always a bit of a queue of stiffs waiting to head underground.

Hence, it's been a good couple of weeks since Charlie drifted off to eternal slumber, but the day of his funeral is now finally arrived.

And so here we is again in the car park of the Maculate Concept, where once more the crooked villainy of Brighton and South London is all assembled to pay due respects, or otherwise…

Yes, they is all here; the various collections of crumbling codger villains, many what you has seen before. And, yes, they is all dressed up again in funereal black - brings out the lack of colour in their faces – as they stand about, nodding, shaking, chatting reverentially.

Apart from the lack of a genuine corpse, what is also slightly unusual about this funeral, is that you got the three representatives of the ex-trouble and strife department of Charlie. All standing together, talking in nasty whispers. United - as is traditional in these ex-wife situations - in their animosity towards the most recent model. In this case Kyrstee.

Poor Kyrstee. Heart of gold that girl.

And Kyrstee does looks like the genuine tearful spouse. What with all that black velvet, and the veiled hat. Well looks the part, she does. And Reg? Well, he's also in his formal funereals: dark suit, crisp white shirt and black tie. You know, standing alongside, comforting Kyrstee. Well, it's what Charlie would have wanted.

Then here comes Lenny and Chen arriving on their mobility scooters, and Spandau Barry too with old Hadley on his shoulder, parking up the Savanna. How old is that parrot anyhow? Probably live to see all of them to their graves.

And next it's the turn of the *Deepe and Stiff* funeral hearse. Now you might have expected old Charlie to go for the traditional East End Horse and Carriage. You know, a couple of fine coachmen in full regalia, a nice pair of black as black Friesian stallions with all them decorative feathers and what not. Clip clopping all the way down Brighton's London Road to the Church of The Maculate Concept. But given that he's not actually putting in a personal appearance at his own funeral, well, Charlie can afford to be a bit more relaxed. And keep the cost down. So, he's gone and plumped for the classic Bentley. Nice hearse that. Well, touch of class. I say.

And who's that what's bringing up the rear now? Oh yeah, might have guessed, giving it the old tit for tat. You know, just 'cause Charlie arrived late for her brother's not so fond farewell. Yeah, it's Brenda, Paddy and their posse of ne'er-do-wells, swanking it up in four very large saloon cars.

One of them lackeys opens the passenger door and Brenda steps out, all puffed up and permed, but still looking like the two-bit gangster what she is. She makes a bee-line for Chen and Lenny, standing in front of their scooters.

Funny how a soft Irish lilt can sound so disagreeable in the wrong mouth. "I don't know what happened," she says, "or how… or even i̲f̲… But I will tell you this; I'll be watching you lot, just like I'm here watching you all now. And if I hear of any of yous flashing the cash around, or driving around in big fancy cars. Then I'll know. Oh yes, I'll know, and I'll come down on you like a ton of… shite!"

Well, very ill-considered language for a church yard you might say, but that's Brenda Fitzpatrick for you. No respect. Lenny, Chen and Spandau Barry don't half look nervous. Even old

Hadley's a bit jittery. Well, Brenda likes to put people on edge. But she's so used to it, she don't pick up on any vibe out of the ordinary.

"I'm sorry for your loss," she says and marches off into the chapel. Walking a bit better now, is Brenda. Well, had that cheese and onion sorted at last.

The Bentley is unloading, and it's Charlie's old crew, Mickey, Coffee-mate, Bas, Trevor, Pinkie and Big Albie what will carry the coffin. Some of their kids is helping too, of course. Well, that cash is heavy. That's a lot of pall bearers. Let's hope they don't get in each other's way. I mean, the last thing we want is that coffin tumbling open and old Father Scanlon thinking he's got a nice little contribution towards the Maculate Concept upkeep.

And well, happily, that coffin makes its way safely down the aisle, and is soon perched on the supports at the front. It's time now for old Father Scanlon, resplendent once more in flamboyant funereal vestments, to report on his progress towards full-blown dementia.

"Ah now, poor, old Charlie Crystal," he says. "A fine man, indeed. A criminal - professional - and a good Catholic… Well, a Catholic. And sure, not the first to combine those two qualities. And didn't I just go and hear his last confession myself, sure, just a few weeks ago?"

Some of the congregation sit up; well, this might be interesting.

"And I can tell you this," goes on the priest, "for I'm not breaking any of the sacred Confessional Secrets Act here, but I can tell you that I expected a little more. You know, for a man who spent so much of his life on the wanted list, on the run, and in prison, his confession… Well, it came as a little bit of a disappointment. Still, he has made his peace with his Maker and didn't he just go and buy the good Lord a couple of fine examples of the Blessed Virgin and old St Anthony himself."

Father Scanlon takes a look at his new statues. And very nice they is too. "Lovely," he says. "That'll stand him in good stead with The Almighty, I'm sure."

The priest then turns his attention directly to his nice new St Anthony statue. "Now you just mind and get on with your work, Anthony. There's a brand-new pair of bifocals hiding somewhere in the Chapel House, and I'm still waiting to hear…"

There's not much more to say about the funeral. It passes off peacefully enough. A few loud tuts and stage laughs from Paddy and crew at them eulogies. Well, 'specially Trevor's; '*I don't see what could possibly go wrong for Charlie at them Pearly Gates*'. Yeah Trev, maybe so. I mean, I wouldn't be surprised if Charlie had already gone and switched them Pearly Gates locks, you know, to afford easy access. Or who knows, maybe that old Father Scanlon's Plenary Indulgence card has actually done the trick for him. You know, been money well spent.

We'll never know.

Anyhows, the funeral passes off with no violence. And given that old Father Scanlon has just got his hands on a couple of brand-new saintly sculptures, well, that must come as a bit of a relief.

So, having shaken his thurible and filled the air with thick incense; went a bit too far, that, 'specially with Trevor having asthma, or is it COPD? And having splashed the coffin with holy water all the way from Lourdes via a pious parishioner's camper van, Father Scanlon stands up at the pulpit and makes his final funereal announcement.

"Now," he says, "I know it's not for everyone, but those of your wishing to join the grieving…" - he cops a disapproving look at Kyrstee - "… grieving concubine, at the Crematorium to say your final farewells, well, you are very welcome to follow the funeral procession on foot or in your cars."

And very shortly, outside, Kyrstee and Reg climb into the first black limo what is to head up the funeral cortège.

There's a sudden realisation what comes over Lenny, Chen and Spandau as they come out the Maculate Concept.

Lenny turns to Chen. "Crematorium?! Wait a minute, wait a minute, Chen! Did he just say Crematorium?"

He did.

"Oo-er," says Hadley, picking up on the anxious vibe.

So, Lenny scoots over to that black limo - the one with Kyrstee and Reg in the back - and knocks on the window. Kyrstee rolls it down.

"No, Kyrstee," he says. "No. Not the crematorium. Charlie's being buried. He wants to spend eternity in that woodland burial site!"

"And he will Lenny," says Kyrstee, a soft smile of lighting up her face. "He will. I'm going to scatter his ashes there myself, and have a nice little cherry tree planted in his name. He loved cherries, Charlie."

"No! But he wanted to be buried, Kyrstee. You have to bury him."

"Oh, old Charlie don't mind, Len. He as good as told me when we went up there to that woodland place together. No, I don't like the thought of him been eaten up by all them little worms over the years… It's horrible. I'd have nightmares, Len. I would. And anyway, it's much more hygienic, you know, cremation. Ecological too… No, we can scatter his ashes together if you like. You, me, Chen and Barry. Just like Charlie would have wanted…"

She rolls up the window and off that car goes, leaving a dumbstruck Lenny staring into the middle distance, as people so often do in similar situations.

...

## Chapter 20

The crematorium is just up the road from the Maculate Concept, and here we is now. Charlie's crew, including Lenny, Chen, Spandau Barry and the doc is all seated down one side; well, Lenny and Chen is parked in the side aisle of course. And sitting opposite, is Brenda, Paddy and all their lot. And look who's sneaked in at the back. It's old misery guts himself; Sergeant Les Misèrables. What's he doing here? Come to make sure Charlie goes up in flames, I should think.

I wonder what he would think if he knew the truth of all this, old Les. You know, that Charlie did actually cook that corn on the cob what the sarky Sarg joked about. And got away with it. Well, sort of... I mean, given that we got several million pounds from old Charlie's criminal endeavours what is about to be cremated, well, I reckon that sad fact alone might just confirm the Sargeant's long-held low opinion of Mr Charles Maurice Joseph Crystal.

For yes, that lovely coffin full of cash is just sitting there - ready to be roasted – sitting up on a raised conveyer belt counter, bang in the front of them all. Tantalising. Touching distance. And they's all got a vested interest in what's inside. Though half the congregation is blissfully unaware why.

I suppose you might say it's a case of so near yet so far.

I mean, what can Charlie's crew do? They can't do nothing, not with Brenda and the Old Bill there.

Even Doc Walker, clever as he is, all he does is give it the old rumble, rumble.

Father Scanlon is standing at a wooden lectern, back in his black cassock now he is, holding forth. "Ah now,' he says, talking to the coffin. "Remember man; earth to earth, dust to dust, ashes to ashes. Though in your case Charlie Crystal, you know, cremation and so forth, the emphasis is on the ashes…"

Then the old priest looks over to the band. "Right," he says, "over to you, lads."

And look, there's that purple velvet mob again. You remember them. This time - I mean, they do like their Booker T, that band, don't they? - so this time, it's *Hip Hug-Her*.

Nice tune, that. Captures a mood of... well, inescapable inevitability, you might say. Yeah, just exactly how most crooks end their days. So, it's very appropriate you might say, and a pleasant enough accompaniment too, as all the congregation stare at that coffin with their mixed emotions.

Them red velvet crematorium curtains with the gold frill, you know the ones - the ones what really belong in an old TV game show - well, they opens up automatically. And then they close in exactly the same way behind, as that coffin of cash slides along the conveyor belt and heads into the flames.

Tacky, I know. But that's crematoriums for you.

Yes, it's curtains folks.

...

# Chapter 21

Curtains for some, but not for everyone…

'Cause, well… I wonder, has you ever been down that Costa Del Crime? You know, Marbella and all that. Where all them crooks used to swan off to in the 70s and 80s, just so as they could avoid extradition. Well, of course, it's Morocco these days, innit? Not quite the same.

Anyhows, down there, on the old Costa del Crime, it's warm and the light is bright too. What with the sun shining down, that pale blue sky, not a cloud in sight, and that reflecting, sparkling sea. I mean, like some of them old fugitive villains, you know, in the summer, they used to say that the light was so bright, they had to wear shades in bed just to sleep at night.

And to get to my here-and-now point, it's a bright light and warm sun what shines down on a lovely Spanish villa right there, on the Golden Mile. You know, just between Marbella and Puerto Banus. Just lovely.

That villa's got the sea views, private grounds, nice big wall to keep out any riff raff what might be down on a day trip from Torremolinos. Touch of seclusion, but at the same time not too far from a bit of night life, if that's what you want. It's also got the swimming pool; mosaic floor with the nymph on the dolphin and all that. The gardens; pink, purple and white bougainvillea, mimosa trees, manicured lawn, that squidgy bouncy grass, you know, what you get down there. Very comfortable on the bare feet. Not so good for the golf, they say.

And look, there's a Range Rover Evoque parked up in the drive. 'Ere, haven't we seen that car before?

We have. 'Cause inside that villa - would you Adam and Eve it? - there's Kyrstee, in her bedroom, sitting at a dressing table, looking in the mirror.

Funny, but a lot of folks in this country won't have dressing tables no more. You know, they say they is old-fashioned. But they's still very popular in Spain.

Looks like Kyrstee's getting ready for a big night out. Reg is in there too, sitting on an enormous circular bed right in the middle of the room. Magnolia white satin sheets and pillows and all. Looks very comfortable. They's quietly chatting to one another.

"D'you think I should wear these ones tonight then, Reg?" says Kyrstee, holding up a nice pair of gold and pearl earrings. Stone me! Them's the ones what Trevor stole!

"Oh, I don't know"' says Reg. "I like them all, Kyrstee."

"Yeah, so do I, Precious. But I like these ones 'specially," says Kyrstee with that perfect smile. "They got a special meaning too, and I mean, well, they're antiques, you know. Yeah, I think these probably go best with the ivory and blue dress, don't you?" She holds up one of them pearl earrings to her lovely little ear.

"I think you look beautiful whatever, Kyrstee," says Reg, climbing off the bed and standing behind her, hands on her bare shoulders, looking at her lovely face in the mirror.

"Awe... Precious..." says Kyrstee, and she puts the ear-rings on and stands up. "Here, zip me up," she says.

Well, it's tempting, innit? I mean, a beautiful woman like Kyrstee, all done up for a night out like. Yeah, pull that zip down in the other direction, you might say. But credit where credit is due, and young Reg, well, he resists - for the time being anyhows - and zips her up. In the process he gives her a nice little kiss on nape of her soft neck. She looks just the ticket in that ivory and blue dress. And them pearl earrings? Well, they do set it all off very nicely.

He's still standing behind her, Reg, looking straight at her reflection in the mirror. "When did you first know then?" he says, a note of curiosity in his voice. "When… I mean… Of course, I knew old Charlie was up to something but…"

"When?" says Kyrstee.

Well, best if I explains all this by way of a flashback, I reckon.

…

Cast your mind back to that mortuary at *Deepe and Stiff*. It's a dark evening, and there's Reg and Kyrstee arriving in a large white van; looks like any old white van. Except it's full of black bags stuffed with newspapers and a bundle of big empty green recycling bags. We're talking colour coding here, you don't want no rookie errors.

They go inside and shake hands with that mortuary attendant, Clive. Then, with his full connivance, they remove all them bundles of cash from that coffin, and place them in the green recycling bags.

Reg, 'cause they is well heavy now, then carries these green bags back to the van, what he has already emptied of the black bags. 'Cause, what do they go and do then? They only go and fill up that coffin with a load of old newspapers. That's exactly what they do. Very crafty.

I tell you it's ironic too. 'Cause one of them newspapers is a recent copy of the *Brighton Evening Argus* what carries the headline; '*Daring Robbery in Brighton Lanes. Thieves vanish into thin air with estimated £8M*'.

Well, them newspapers is always exaggerating.

Having done the dirty then, mostly in silence, Kyrstee turns to Clive. "Can I see him?" she says, sweetly.

They go across to the fridge and Clive slides Charlie out one more time. He pulls back the thin white cotton sheet and old Charlie Crystal's face is revealed.

Well, that's not how I remember him. You know, his face, when Brenda clapped her eyes on him. I mean, he looks terrified now. His face is all twisted and knotted.

Kyrstee looks back at Clive, puzzled. He shrugs his shoulders. "Rigor mortis," he says with a shake of the head, "does some terrible things."

Still, Kyrstee leans over and gives old Charlie a kiss on his stone-cold forehead. "Awe… Don't you worry about me, Charlie," she says. "I'll be just fine."

The van is now loaded up and Reg climbs back into the driver's seat. Kyrstee, what is closing up the rear - without any apparent difficulty it would seem - hands one green bag to Clive. He tilts his head and raises an eyebrow. Well, you get his drift. Kyrstee smiles and hands him another green bag. Well, she's nothing if not generous, albeit with other people's money.

A big grin lights up Clive's face. First time for everything, I suppose. Blimey, that's a cruel set of gnashers he's got in there, old Clive. Looks like a collection of old headstones what's all tumbled over in a neglected graveyard. One of two of them Hampsteads of his is actually covered in lichen if I'm not mistaken. Never clocked that before.

Ahh… That's why… Yeah… That explains it, you know, the absence of any spontaneous bon-amie in that mournful mortuary attendant. Well, never you mind, Clive. Leastways, now you can afford a nice smile, courtesy of some proper professional dental work. 'Cause that can be quite expensive.

Anyhows, all done and dusted, Kyrstee climbs into the passenger seat and Reg drives off in the moonlight.

...

Back in Spain, Kyrstee turns around from the dressing table to face Reg. "Hmm? D'you mean when did I know about the plan, the robbery, and all that money in the coffin?"

"Yeah," says Reg with a nod.

"Silly. I always knew. Anyway, I'm sure Charlie would approve, he was always a ladies' man, after all."

Reg is impressed. Well, who wouldn't be? "You're beautiful, <u>and</u> clever." he says.

"Awe. You don't half say the nicest things, Precious."

They hold hands and head out to the Range Rover. Should be a good night.

And it's always nice to have a happy ending, innit?

...

Printed in Dunstable, United Kingdom